WISHES IN WINTER

THE WICKED WINTERS

BOOK 3.5

SCARLETT SCOTT

Happily Ever After Books

Wishes in Winter

The Wicked Winters Book 3.5

PROLOGUE

LONDON, SPRING 1813

*T*he dark night was lit with a bevy of twinkling, ethereal stars, if one bothered to look. Lady Lydia Brownlow was the sort of female who *did* look. She had studied astronomy under the auspices of her late and most beloved grandpapa, and she recognized the delights of Cassiopeia and Andromeda better than most.

She inhaled deeply of the fragrant earth and intricate gardens about to renew with the unfurling of the new season. Flowers would blossom. The earth would warm. Another round of parties and routs and musicales would unfold. One more season of enduring her mother's pointed sniping about the arts of a lady and her father's beleaguered attempts to get her to set her cap at an eligible gentleman.

Endless and unwanted, all of it, save spring's vibrant renaissance. But here, at last, in the calm of the Earl of Havenhurst's gardens, she could steal a slice of solitude. Here was a space in which she could be herself, look upon the stars and think of the man who taught her how to gaze into the heavens and see a world beyond her sheltered sphere.

Her heart gave a pang, the prick of tears making the glittering formation above go blurry. How she missed Grand-papa. Her nose began to run, and she sniffled. Oh, bother. She had already risked her mother's wrath by escaping from the evening's festivities. If she returned looking a fright…

"Mother will have my head on a pike," she muttered.

"I do hope not," drawled a low, familiar voice just over her shoulder.

With a gasp, she spun about, hand over her fluttering heart as if mere pressure could somehow still its foolish pace. It would not, for *that* voice—with its deep, velvety rasp seemingly crafted by the Lord himself to make all females swoon—always had the same humiliating effect upon her.

In the shadows of the garden, she could not discern his chiseled features, though the silvery bath of moonlight washed his face in just enough light to confirm her mortification was complete. Of all the people in the crush of Lord Havenhurst's ballroom, why did it have to be the Duke of Warwick who came upon her when she was sniffling and talking to herself in the dark?

She sniffed again, hoping she did not have any tears leaking from her eyes or, even worse, an unladylike ribbon of snot descending from her nose. "Warwick, what are you doing out here?"

Lydia did not bother to hide her vexation, for if she disliked anything more than someone sneaking up behind her, it was surely her unfortunate reaction to the duke. Whenever she entered his rarified presence, her heart beat like the frantic wings of a bird and a heavy, tingling sensation stole through her. A reaction that was equal parts disconcerting and unwanted.

"The same could be asked of you." He took a step closer, canting his head as the tips of his gloved fingers found her chin and asserted enough gentle pressure to tilt her face to his. "The devil. Are you crying, Freckles?"

Freckles.

The old, childhood nickname ought not disturb her.

Indeed, she ought to remind him that she was Lady Lydia, no longer the wayward girl, five years his junior, who snuck away from her grim governess to fish with him and her brother, much to their mutual irritation. As a girl, she had been hopelessly dazzled by him, dreaming of the day when she would be old enough and pretty enough for him to notice her. For him to look at her the way he did her gorgeous elder sister Mary and Mary's equally graceful, charming friends.

But as she had grown older and the naïveté of her youth dissipated, she had accepted that such a day would never arrive. Here she stood, a woman grown, resplendent in her white evening gown, roses in her hair, and for all that, still a bluestocking about to be left forever on the shelf.

Still Freckles rather than Lady Lydia. Still a creature worthy of Warwick's pity. And though her girlish fancy for him had matured into a hardened acceptance that he would never look upon her as a woman, her cheeks still flamed under his intense regard.

This would not do. She squared her shoulders, recalling she had seen him dancing with Lady Felicity Drummond not half an hour before, a true diamond of the first water. A handsome couple they made, Lady Felicity's golden curls a rich contrast to Warwick's mahogany locks.

"I am not crying, Warwick," she snapped, taking a step in retreat so that she could inhale without breathing in the decadent masculine scent of his shaving soap, and so that he no longer held her chin captive. "I do not cry."

He ignored her obvious desire for space, stalking forward in what she knew to be gleaming Hessians, for she had admired them and his strong thighs and calves as she'd watched him dance earlier.

3

"Is it a gentleman?" An edge underscored his tone. "Only give me a name, and I will meet him at dawn."

She frowned. He sounded oddly sincere, perhaps even angry at the imagined offender. "There is no gentleman, and I was not crying. Now, do go away before someone comes upon us. I should like to be alone, precisely as I was, before your unwanted interruption."

Being Warwick, he ignored her. "I am not one to put in my oar, Freckles, but your eyes were glistening in the moonlight, and you are out here alone, and I distinctly heard a sniffle."

She sighed. "Very well. If you must know, I was thinking of my grandfather."

"Then there is no need for me to assist some jackanapes with sticking his spoon in the wall tomorrow?" he asked gently.

Was it her imagination, or had he drifted nearer? She could once more smell him, and while her inner fool applauded any and all proximity to the Duke of Warwick, her sense of reason most assuredly did not.

"No, though you do have a way of phrasing things, Warwick. Are you as cow-handed with all the ladies, or is this a special treatment reserved for myself alone?"

"I would not duel for any other lady's honor save my mother's."

His pronouncement filled her with shock and then a deep, suffusing warmth that she could not contain. It was as if the sun had suddenly appeared in the garden, burning away the night. But, no. This was Warwick before her, Corinthian, prime marriage mart prize, the most handsome man in London, and notorious Lothario. He did not mean what he said. Very likely, it was the sort of thing he said to every lady.

She swallowed, tamping down the stupid, fugitive joy in

4

her heart. "Do not attempt to cozen me, Warwick. I am immune to your wiles."

"I admired your grandfather greatly," he said, startling her with the thread of tenderness in his voice. "He was a fine man, and he always praised your keen mind."

Lydia bit her lip to stifle the sudden sob that threatened to tear from her throat and further shame her. One year and two months had come and gone since Grandpapa's passing, and yet his loss remained as fresh as yesterday. He alone had encouraged her pursuit of knowledge, but to hear he had openly sung her praises to others…why, it touched her deeply.

She sniffled again. "He was a very fine man indeed."

Long, strong fingers claimed hers, and she felt the shock and the heat of it through her gloves. "You may cry, Freckles. I shan't think any less of you, and I promise to defend you against any and all attempts by your mother to slay you and put your severed head on a pike."

A startled laugh escaped her, and she found herself squeezing his fingers. She could not seem to summon her resistance, not when he was being so kind and it felt as if the years and distance between them had fallen away. Once, when she'd trailed Warwick and her brother Rand, she had taken a tumble whilst chasing a butterfly, straight into the pond where they fished. She had been unable to swim, and Warwick dove in after her, plucked her from the watery depths with ease and carried her like a waterlogged babe to the shore.

Why would she think of that long-ago day now, when she had not for many years?

She must shake herself from this madness, turn and leave before she said or did something she would forever regret. Here, in the moonlight, they were Freckles and Warwick. Back in the glittering light of the ballroom, they would return to being strangers, she the bluestocking wallflower and he, the sought-after bachelor.

"Thank you for your kind offer, Your Grace," she said solemnly, extricating her fingers from his. "But my earlier worries aside, I do not truly think my mother will murder me unless I linger here in the gardens with a hardened rake such as yourself. I really must return before my absence is noted."

She turned to flee, but was stilled by her name on his lips. At long last.

"Lady Lydia."

Lydia stopped, her back rigid, but did not dare face him. "Yes?"

"You do not dance often. Why?" He sounded genuinely perplexed.

She closed her eyes, a fresh wave of humiliation washing over her. Could he be that obtuse? "I am not asked. Gentlemen do not, I find as a general rule, enjoy dancing with ladies who are taller and smarter than they are."

"Ah." He had drifted closer. She felt his presence behind her, awareness tingling down her spine. "You are fortunate then, that I am taller than you, and I do not take exception to a lady who is my intellectual equal or better. Save a dance for me."

A foreign thrill swept over her, pooling low in her belly, before self-preservation superseded and she did the only thing she could think of in that moment. She hurried away from him, away from his delicious voice, and far away from the garden of temptation.

CHAPTER 1

DECEMBER, 1813

*A*listair had not dragged himself to Abingdon Hall in Oxfordshire for the punch. The flavor was middling, not nearly as sickeningly sweet as orgeat. Nor had he come for the pine boughs and sprigs of mistletoe. He had not even come for the endless diversions. Or for Christmas.

He scoured the ballroom in search of his quarry.

He was more than aware that, as the Duke of Warwick, he was one of the most eligible catches of the *beau monde*. Thankfully, within the select ranks of Mr. Devereaux Winter and Lady Emilia Winter's Christmas country house party, he felt less like a fox surrounded by a pack of slavering hounds than he ordinarily did. Even if it was no secret the reason for the fête was to secure noble matches for Mr. Winter's five sisters.

It was fortunate indeed, for he had grown tired of the female pursuit which had dogged him all his life. Caps had been thrown at him, ad nauseam, nearly since he'd been in leading strings. He was accustomed to feminine wiles, stares, the attempts of matchmaking mothers. In his youth, that admiration had swelled his pride. Now, at seven-and-twenty, it left him feeling hollow. Searching for something elusive.

Searching for *her*.

Or, to be specific, for his Freckles, dedicated bluestocking, sister to his very best friend, and the one woman who, of all the ladies of his acquaintance—which were nigh *legion*—was the only woman with whom he would face the hangman's noose. *Er*, the only woman he would wed. And wed he must. With as much haste as he could politely manage. Time was no longer a commodity he could afford to squander.

"Are you certain she is not hiding in her chamber reading a book, Aylesford?" he growled at the friend by his side, frustration getting the better of him.

"Who, are you looking for, Warwick?" Rand, Viscount Aylesford, took a sip of his punch and grimaced. "Devil take it with the swill they serve at these country affairs. Where is blue ruin when one needs it? And why the hell did I allow myself to be forced into attendance here at such a tedious affair?"

"Blue ruin is decidedly *de trop* on the marriage mart." He ignored his friend's question and flicked a glance over the glittering lords and ladies assembled, seeking sleek auburn curls. "I'm afraid you will have to suffer the punch or go dry, unless you can convince Mr. Winter to open his stores of liquor for you."

"The marriage mart." Rand shuddered. "If my dragon grandmother has her way, I shall not be long upon it. Remind me why I am here when I have no interest in the parson's mousetrap."

Rand was a notorious rakehell and ne'er-do-well. Alistair had not been far from his footsteps over the last few years. Together, they had lost themselves in drink and quim aplenty. But circumstances had altered for Alistair.

Vastly.

And he could no longer afford to live the life he once had. Literally.

He kept his tone bored, attempting to cloak the unrest stealing through him lest his friend grow suspicious. "Because the dowager has decreed you must wed if you wish to inherit Tyre Abbey. Not to mention your mother and sister are in attendance."

There. That ought to be enough substance to distract Rand from the fact that Alistair, his best friend, wanted his sister with a desperation so strong he felt it in his teeth. For now.

Of course, he would need to tell Rand the truth soon enough. Perhaps even tonight, if Freckles ever deigned to appear, for he meant to make his intentions known to her as expediently as possible. His friend would not object to the match, he thought.

Just as long as Rand did not discover how perilously near to ruin he was.

"How could I forget?" Rand asked. "Family duty is a bugbear. Thank Christ Hertford suggested the idea of a feigned betrothal. I ought to have thought of it myself."

"Have you convinced Miss Winter to agree to your plan?" he asked, still searching for his quarry.

She had been avoiding him all Season long, since the night he'd found her in the gardens at Havenhurst's ball, which had been the very same evening that he'd realized the answer to his predicament had been before him all along. But not only had she denied him his dance by pleading a headache to her mother and leaving the affair prematurely, she had also thwarted him at every turn thereafter.

"Not yet." Rand's tone was confident.

And why should it not be? He was a rake who always got what he wanted.

Alistair had been too, once. Now, what he wanted—and

9

needed—most remained elusive. Freckles and blunt, in precisely that order.

When he had attempted to seek her out at the Bodley musicale, she had disappeared into the lady's withdrawing room. He had dined with her family, and she had been absent, with some unconvincing excuse made on her behalf. Nearly every attempt he made to cross paths with her at society events had resulted in her skillful evasion.

To make matters worse, he had learned from Rand that, under pressure from their parents, the Duke and Duchess of Revelstoke, Freckles was expected to make a match before she retired to the shelf forever. The duke was prepared to send her off to become companion to the Marchioness of Bond and her half dozen ill-mannered corgis.

Alistair gritted his teeth at the thought of Freckles becoming the lackey of a well-documented curmudgeon like the Marchioness of Bond. Freckles was not meant to fade into the background.

Why not her?

It was the question that had struck him as he'd gazed upon her in the moonlight, noting how very lovely she was, with her tall, lissome form and auburn hair, her retroussé nose kissed with freckles and her stubborn chin. The tears and sadness in her eyes had made him long to take her into his arms, and that protective surge, the urgent need to comfort her, had taken him by surprise.

How foolish of him to never have considered Freckles before, when now it seemed impossible to imagine any other lady fulfilling the role he would have her claim. He needed to marry, and if he must have anyone, he would have her. Freckles was loyal and intelligent, and though she never strayed from speaking her mind, he found he rather admired that trait. He could do no better in his future wife.

Of course, there was also the matter of her impressive

dowry, and that could not be overlooked, as it, too, was quite necessary.

"You will persuade her of the wisdom of your strategy in no time, I am certain," he forced himself to say, his mind traveling back to Freckles once more, as it invariably did.

"Damned inconvenient, all these fortune hunters sniffing about," Rand said dismissively.

Fortune hunters.

The phrase made him stiffen. His sire's staggering obligation was not a topic he preferred to think about. The mere thought of the former duke gambling himself into oblivion before putting a pistol in his mouth filled him with an incapacitating rage. Alistair was on the brink of penury, just as many of the lords in attendance were, drawn by the lure of the Winter sisters and their massive dowries.

But unlike the others, he was not attending the house party to snare a share of the Winter fortune.

He was here to snare Lady Lydia Brownlow, whose dowry, while far surpassed by the Winters' wealth, was immense on its own. Revelstoke was rich as Croesus, and in an effort to marry off Freckles this Season so the younger daughter, Cecily, could debut, he had been bandying about the value of her dowry everywhere he could.

All London knew marrying her would result in a sizable fortune. It wasn't the sole reason Alistair wanted to make Freckles his duchess, but he was uncomfortably aware his best friend may have cause to disagree should he ever discover the extent of his father's debts.

He very much did not want anyone—let alone Rand—interfering with getting what he wanted. And what he wanted the more he thought upon it was Freckles, who smelled of spring violets and possessed gray eyes that shimmered with intelligence, whose lush mouth seemed undeniably created for kissing.

For *his* kisses, to be precise.

His alone.

He felt suddenly, fiercely possessive of her. He did not know what it was about her—he had tried to understand the force of his newfound, troublesome feelings without success —but somewhere betwixt that moonlit garden and this very moment, he had become determined to make Lady Lydia Brownlow his.

If he was honest, it had begun before the Havenhurst ball. He could still recall the way she had felt in his arms the one and only time he had danced with her, and the moment when he had gazed into her upturned face and noticed her eyes contained vivid flecks of blue. Awareness had sparked between them even then. She had called him a rogue when he had complimented her dress, which had been a pink affair wholly unsuited to her personality. A strange stirring had occurred inside him.

Ridiculous, he had told himself at the time. *This is Freckles.*

And yet, that same thing had not moved one whit from its spot, lodged firmly in the vicinity of the heart he would have sworn he did not own. When he had called upon her following the ball, she had muttered something that sounded suspiciously like "jackanapes" when he had bowed before her and kissed her gloved hand. He had yearned to keep her trapped in his grip, to haul her away from their unwanted audience, and kiss her senseless.

Devil take it, his cock was going hard, right here in the midst of the ballroom, before all and sundry. There was no hope for it—he must confess to Rand now, before he waded any deeper into these dangerous waters. He cleared his throat, deciding there was no delicate way to inform one's oldest and best friend that one lusted after his sister and intended to marry her. "Rand, there is something I must discuss with you."

"Dear God, Warwick. If you intend to get serious, I need a drink that isn't more suited to babes and ladies than men fully grown." Rand downed the dregs of his punch in a final gulp, curling his lip after he swallowed. "Gads. I cannot believe I stooped so low as to consume such rot."

Alistair didn't blame him. There was nothing he would like so much as a fine glass of port or a redoubtable whisky, but in their current environs, no such respite was forthcoming. "I am afraid that I must be serious."

"Blast, there is my sister and my mother," Rand said distractedly. "Would you mind terribly if we greeted them? Father has sworn this house party is Lydia's last chance to find a match so Cecily may come out, and perhaps if you show interest in her, it will inspire some of these clods to ask her for a dance, if nothing else."

He clenched his jaw. "Hold, Rand. Let us be clear: there is no lady I would prefer to greet more than Fr-Lady Lydia. Her intellect is far superior to every other lady of my acquaintance. Indeed, she is every other lady's superior in all ways, including loveliness, for hers is a beauty that shines from within. No others can hope to hold a candle to it."

He meant every word. In fact, he would have liked to have said more. Freckles was not merely beautiful. She was vibrant. She was animated. Being in her presence was akin to standing beneath the heated summer sky—glorious, and yet one could so easily get burned. Rand was his friend, yes, but Alistair did not like the manner in which he spoke of Freckles, as though she were the recipient of social alms. Someone to be pitied, rather than worshipped.

And Alistair meant to worship her as soon as possible. With his mouth and his tongue. But that was certainly not the sort of thing a man said to his best friend when the lady in question was his best friend's sister.

Rand gave him a questioning look. "My sister? Christ,

Warwick. Tell me you are not waxing eloquent over *my sister*. If you are, I shall have to challenge you to a duel on principle."

His cheekbones went hot. How mortifying. He found himself gazing beyond his friend, to the place where—at long last—Freckles stood with her turban-wearing mother, the Duchess of Revelstoke. Freckles wore an ivory gown embroidered with roses that hugged her curvaceous figure and emphasized her luscious breasts.

"I do not *wax eloquent*," he forced himself to say through a mouth gone suddenly dry. "Ever. But by all means, do let us greet the Duchess of Revelstoke and Lady Lydia."

Rand grinned at him then. "I am joking about the duel, old chap. If you do want to marry Lyd, I should be relieved. One less bugbear. There is no other gentleman I would be more pleased to see her wed."

Alistair's gut clenched as he wondered if his friend would feel the same way if he knew the truth.

CHAPTER 2

*T*he last man she had expected to see at the country house party being held by Lady Emilia Winter and her husband Mr. Devereaux Winter was the Duke of Warwick.

Lydia had been avoiding him with great success for the last few months, but as she watched him bearing down upon her with her brother in tow, she found herself frozen, unable to escape. Why had Rand not told her Warwick would be in attendance?

Because he had likely been too busy with his paramour of the moment.

Her beloved brother was a libertine of the first—and worst—order.

"Warwick, for instance," her mother continued in the midst of the matrimonial prospects diatribe Lydia had been doing her utmost to ignore, "would make an excellent match. Though I daresay he will ask for Lady Felicity's hand, or perhaps even one of the dreadful Winter girls, he has not yet done so. It is not too late for you. You must smile, and you must endeavor to never speak of any of your odd notions.

Do not mention that *star* poppycock, I beg. You could have a coronet. Just think of it, a coronet, my dear. Here he comes. Oh, do smile, Lydia. *Smile*."

Her mother said the last through gnashed teeth.

Lydia ignored her, steeling herself against the weakness a man as breathtakingly magnetic as the Duke of Warwick produced in her. She would remain indifferent. He was a rake like her brother. A flirt. He was not interested in her, though it occasionally amused him to act as if he were.

She was not the mouse to his cat. Indeed, she was no mouse at all. She would far prefer to be a mastiff, chasing his cat away where he could no longer torment her. Up a tree, perhaps.

As he reached her, she fixed him with her sternest glare.

A smile flirted with his sensual mouth and he bowed with his inimitable, sleek grace. Why, he even moved like a cat. "Your Grace, Lady Lydia."

Not Freckles this evening, then. But she ought not to be surprised, and so she squelched the throbbing surge of awareness that made her pulse leap. Of course, he would not dare to refer to her in such improper fashion whilst in public and before her mother. As he straightened, the full effect of him slammed into her with the force of a blow.

Had all the air been stolen from the ballroom? And was it her imagination at work, or did his gaze slip to her lips for a heartbeat before rising? He was insufferably handsome, his jaw pronounced, his nose straight, his lips full and sinfully carnal, his eyes blue and bright, cheekbones high. His dark, tousled hair only added to the allure.

In short, he was so beautiful it made her ache in odd places. Places she had never had cause to notice before him.

Pity that he was a rascal who preferred witless ninnies like Lady Felicity to ladies of wit and substance. Not to mention, that he had witnessed her doused in pond water, along with an innumerable series of unladylike events over the years of their acquaintance.

"Lydia," her mother ground out, *sotto voce*, as she pasted a beaming smile to her face and curtsied like a schoolgirl.

Apparently, no lady was immune to Warwick in his superfine coat, buff breeches, and immaculate white cravat tied in the American fashion. She had to admit he cut a debonair figure, and he quite took her breath simply by standing before her. It was not fair for a man to be so glorious to look upon.

Belatedly aware she stood mooning over Warwick as though she too were besotted by his good looks—she was *not*, she vowed—she swept into a curtsy. "Your Grace."

His solemn gaze lingered upon her, intent and seeking, and the smile that had seemed poised to dawn over his features did not come to fruition. "Would you do me the honor of dancing with me, Lady Lydia?"

"You need not dance with me," she said, her meaning clear.

She would not accept his pity.

"Oh, la, Lady Lydia." Mother laughed as if she had just delivered the cleverest sally. "You do possess the most original *sens de l'humour*. Of course, the duke needs to dance with you."

"No, he does not," Lydia denied.

The Duchess of Revelstoke's gaze could have pierced the Spanish armada as she glared at Lydia. "Yes," she insisted, keeping an unnatural smile affixed to her lips. "He does."

"Do not go into high dudgeon, Mother. This is deuced awkward." Rand's brows snapped together as he looked from Lydia to Warwick. "Warwick has agreed to dance with Lyd as a favor, in hopes it may encourage other suitors, which she is already woefully wanting."

Their mother's face went scarlet. Lydia's stomach

dropped to somewhere in the vicinity of her delicate slippers. She knew her brother did not realize he was occasionally an unfeeling oaf, or that he was making a cake of her before the last man in England that she wanted to think her a hopelessly on-the-shelf spinster.

But he was.

The thought gave her pause. Why should she care what the Duke of Warwick thought? Of course, she didn't. But for some reason, she was once more ensnared in his gaze, and she swore she saw a glimmer of connection there. A lone spark kindled into a flame within her. She could not look away.

"It would be my honor to dance with you, my lady," the duke insisted quietly, his expression serious.

She did not see pity in his gaze.

"Oh," her mother sighed, sounding breathless—which was utterly absurd, for she had known Warwick since he was in leading strings. "That would be lovely, Warwick. Lady Lydia would be pleased to accept. Would you not, dear?"

What was it about the Christmas season that turned everyone's brain to feathers? Even her own, for she *wanted* to dance with Warwick, she realized. His eyes had not wavered from hers. He waited, patiently, as though her answer was of the greatest import.

"Yes," Lydia accepted. "Of course, I will save you a dance, Duke."

The smile he had been withholding emerged then, and it was broad and mesmerizing and only served to enhance his masculine beauty, which was a feat in itself. She swallowed, thinking back upon that enchanted night in the garden. It could not be possible that he was interested in her. His words returned to her just then.

You are fortunate then, that I am taller than you are, Freckles, and I do not take exception to a lady who is my intellectual equal or better. Save a dance for me.

No. It could not be that the Duke of Warwick, who had only ever seen her as an irritant and a hanger-on, who was the most handsome and eligible bachelor in the *beau monde*, wanted her. That he wanted a bluestocking who was too tall for fashion, too opinionated by far, whose nose was decorated with freckles, and who preferred books to needlework and pianoforte any day.

And yet, his regard told her that he was. Against all odds, the Duke of Warwick looked upon her now in the way a man looked upon a woman. Admiring. Wanting.

The echo of her own fierce need sprang forth from somewhere deep within.

"Thank you, my lady," he told her, his tone soft and admiring. Genuine. With another bow, he turned and left.

Her brother lingered for a moment, his expression contemplative. "Mother." He bowed again. "Lyd." Then he hastened after his friend.

Lydia watched them depart, bemused, attempting to muddle through what to make of this most unsettling development.

"Bravo, daughter," her mother said into the silence, her voice vibrating with maternal pride. "The Duke of Warwick would be quite a feather in your cap."

Yes, he would. But Lydia didn't want a matrimonial prize. Indeed, she didn't even want to be wed. The only reason she stood in the ballroom at that very moment was because her parents had taken her choice away from her. She would do well not to forget that, and above all, not to imagine that a handsome rake like the Duke of Warwick would ever wed the spinster, bluestocking sister of his best friend.

She was Freckles to him, nothing more.

CHAPTER 3

*L*ydia didn't know which fact was more unsettling: that the Duke of Warwick had sought her out each day of the house party thus far or that Jane, her abigail and the woman tasked with guarding her virtue for the moment, had fallen asleep.

They sat in a small parlor in one of the innumerable rooms of Abingdon House. Jane's snores cut into the awkward silence that had descended upon the unexpected *tête-à-tête*. Jane was no longer a stickler for propriety, and while Lydia was fond of her, The abigail's ineffectual presence was more than disconcerting today. It was downright dismaying.

She refused to think of why Jane's tendency to doze off in the corner had never bothered her before now.

Warwick, being the rake he was, noticed the moment he was no longer under scrutiny. "Your maid appears to be sleeping," he observed, his voice low and intimate.

She flushed, keeping her eyes on Jane rather than on Warwick. He was unbearably handsome this morning, and looking upon him stirred a fresh ache deep within her, the sort of ache she had no wish to feel toward him. Most decidedly, an ache that would only land her in trouble from which there was no extrication.

"She is not sleeping," she improvised, lest he develop any wicked ideas. "She is praying."

"Ah, I see." He sounded amused. "Her...piety is to be commended."

Another snore sounded across the room. *Blast.* Lydia firmed her lips. Warwick startled her by rising from his seat and quickly lowering his tall, lean frame at her side on the settee. She stared at his strong thigh, clad in perfectly fitted breeches, touching her gown.

"Warwick, you are crowding me," she grumbled. "It is unseemly for you to be sitting so near. Go back to your chair at once."

He ignored her, as had become his habit. If anything, he seemed to sidle closer. She once again caught a whiff of the decadent scent of his shaving soap, and though it grieved her to admit, she took an extra-deep breath on its account.

"How can it be unseemly when your maid chaperones us so well?" An unrepentant grin livened his voice.

She picked at the fall of her skirt, still not wanting to look upon him, particularly at this proximity. Last evening, he had claimed his dance at the welcome ball, and while there had been little opportunity for private conversation, he had gazed upon her with such concentration whenever their paths had crossed during the minuet, she had nearly tripped over her hem in her distraction. He had looked upon her with a smoldering sort of need that puzzled her as much as it thrilled her, all against her better judgment.

"Jane is an excellent chaperone," she felt obliged to defend. That much, at least, was true. Ordinarily, Lydia had no need of a chaperone at all. Until now. "If she is fatigued, it is merely because I have required her to chaperone me far more in the last few days as I spend time with friends than I ordinarily do. The poor dear is not to be blamed."

His fingers closed over hers, stilling them. "Gentlemen friends, Freckles?"

Something in his tone—an underlying hardness—had her turning her head to meet his gaze, even as she noted that she was once again Freckles rather than Lady Lydia. "Yes, Warwick. *Gentlemen* friends. Your disbelief is quite insulting."

She didn't add that she was surprised herself by the sudden attention. Particularly when she was competing with the lovely—and infamously wealthy—Winter sisters. Then again, her dowry was quite handsome, and the reason for this house party was clear—an entrée for the Winter sisters into polite society.

Many of the gentlemen in attendance were searching for wealthy brides. Likely, her invitation had stemmed from her brother Rand, who, as the heir to a duke, would be quite a prize for any Winter daughter to snare. In spite of his rakish ways.

Little did they know, Rand could not be tamed.

Warwick's jaw clenched, then. "Is your maid this slipshod with all your *friends*?"

Yet another snore, this one louder than the last, rumbled across the room.

Lydia thought for a moment. "Slipshod is rather an unkind choice of word, Warwick. She loves me like a daughter."

The duke gave an indelicate snort that was at odds with his effortless masculine elegance. "I do think granddaughter would be more apt. Listen here, Freckles, if she is snoring through all your suitors, something must be done."

He sounded rather indignant.

Lydia considered him, wondering why on earth he should become so bothered by the somewhat lackluster performance of her maid as a chaperone. Why, it almost seemed as if he were jealous, but that was absurd. Wasn't it? Of course, it was. He was who he was, after all, and she was a wallflower bluestocking who, barring recent developments, almost no one noticed.

Even so, the notion of the sought-after Duke of Warwick being jealous of other suitors vying for her hand pleased her.

"Would you like me to wake Jane?" she asked innocently, baiting him. "After all, your reputation is far more infamous than any of my other suitors, as you say."

"No," he bit out, giving her fingers a squeeze of warning. "Do not wake her. Who are these other suitors you speak of, Freckles?"

"Viscount Tottingham." His was the first name that came to mind.

Warwick scowled. "Tottingham is a coxcomb with a penchant for losing all his blunt at the tables. He is in desperate need of a wealthy bride thanks to his own foibles, which is why he is in attendance here."

This news did not surprise her. She did not care for the viscount, who was the sort of man who never listened to a word spoken that wasn't his own. "He is a reckless gamer, then?"

The duke's brows snapped together. "The worst sort, and not at all deserving of a lady like you as his wife. Who else?"

She tried—unsuccessfully—to squelch the burst of warmth his words ignited within her. *A lady like you.* What could he mean? She wanted to ponder it longer, but he waited expectantly, wishing to hear the rest of her list of gentlemen friends. "The Earl of Fulham."

"Far too old," he said dismissively. "What others?"

"The Marquess of Vale, Viscount Elmhurst, and Sir Stephen Montgomery." All men she did not care for. Not one of them made her body burn as if kissed by flame with the mere act of sitting beside her.

Oh dear. From where had that errant thought come?

"Vale is a rake, Elmhurst is a simpleton, and Sir Stephen is a drunkard," Warwick pronounced. "Is that the lot of them?"

She nodded, aware that he still held her fingers tangled in his grasp and his thumb had begun a lazy exploration of her inner wrist. Circles, of all things, and tantalizing in the most alarming fashion. She should snatch her hand away, and yet she did not wish to. His blue eyes held her entranced. He leaned forward, lowering his head as if to impart a secret.

"You forgot one."

His deep, decadent voice sent an unfamiliar sensation, molten and pleasant, vibrating through her.

The combination of his penetrating regard, nearness, and touch undid her sufficiently enough that she could not follow his logic. She frowned, trying not to become mesmerized by the perfect shape of his mouth or the surprising fullness of his lower lip. Trying not to imagine him setting his lips upon hers.

Kissing her.

"Forgot?" she repeated weakly, thinking for a foolish moment that they were speaking in different languages. Or that he was taking part in a dialogue to which she was not privy.

"Yes." His smile was blinding in its beauty. He flashed even, white teeth. The corners of his eyes crinkled. His dimples revealed themselves. "Me."

She had seen those mesmerizing grooves on many occasions over the years, but she did not recall ever once being the direct cause of them. Or the sole recipient, for that matter. For a moment, they stole her breath. And then she recalled, belatedly, what he had just said.

Lydia gathered her wits. "You are not my suitor, Warwick."

His wicked thumb traveled ever higher, up the sleeve of her prim, white muslin dress, making her pulse leap. "And yet, Freckles, here I sit."

He was jesting, of course. For some reason, he had decided to make her the beneficiary of his rakish games. *Ennui*, perhaps? She supposed he had attended the house party to entertain Rand, who had been quite displeased at the prospect of having to attend. It did not matter. She would not be his source of amusement. She needed to put an end to his nonsense. Immediately.

She snatched her hand from him. "Do not make light of me. I will not be your joke."

"I would not jest about such a thing, my dear." His smile faded, taking with it the dimples that so distracted her. "I am deadly serious when it comes to you."

Surely, she was in the throes of some sort of odd dream. At any moment, she would awake in her bed, and this entire interview with the Duke of Warwick would be revealed for the flight of fancy it undoubtedly was. There was no reason that the handsome rake she had grown up admiring—the same man who had never once looked upon her as a female, who had instead blazed through a series of whispered demi-monde conquests, who had every marriageable lady in London hanging upon his every word and deed—would court her.

Unless…

Her eyes narrowed. "Have you made a wager at your club, Warwick?"

He shook his head slowly. "No, Freckles."

His regard grew in intensity. Why was it so dratted hot in the room? Winter had already set in early, and with it, the unmerciful cold she had come to expect later in the season.

Surely, the source of the warmth could not be the lone fireplace crackling on the far end of the chamber, its flames dying more and more by the minute.

Certainly, it had not seemed this stifling when she had entered. She sidled left, away from Warwick's large, lean form. Perhaps the heat emanating from him was the culprit.

"This is a mission of mercy perpetuated by my brother," she guessed next, trying to ignore how unsettled she felt. "You are pretending to court me to quell the worries of my parents as a favor to Rand."

"Wrong again, Freckles." A rueful half smile curved his sensual mouth. "As much as I consider Rand the brother I never had, I would not play suitor to anyone merely because he asked. Which he most assuredly did not, I assure you."

Her mind whirled, the natural proclivity she'd always possessed for science making her certain there was a logical reason behind Warwick's sudden change. "It cannot be because of my dowry, can it? I understand it is quite generous, but surely there are any other number of ladies with papas who have plump pockets. Or any one of the Misses Winter. They are lovely, all of them, and their fortunes are as large as they are renowned."

"Freckles."

She was not imagining it now. He had tipped his head forward, and his blue gaze burned into hers. His breath skated over her lips, warm and tempting. "Yes?"

"Stop talking." His hand slid into the hair at her nape, and in the next instant, his lips claimed hers.

Lydia went still, adjusting to the strange sensation of a man's mouth upon hers. Not just any man's, but Warwick's. *Oh.* His lips, like his kiss, were surprisingly supple. He kissed her gently at first, a series of light, teasing pecks that left her yearning for more. At last, his tongue swept over the seam of her lips. She gasped, and then everything changed.

He groaned deep within his throat and angled her head to press his advantage. His tongue, bold and plundering, slid inside her mouth. The sensation was decadent. Shocking. Her hands flitted to his broad shoulders, every part of her body alive, aware of him in a way she could not yet comprehend. She breathed him in, tasted him, felt his corded muscles and tempting strength. Despite herself, she leaned forward, her breasts crushing against his chest, and moved her lips in a mimicry of his, kissing him back.

Warwick was kissing her. His tongue was in her mouth. She was clutching and clinging to him like a wanton. Her maid slumbered not ten feet away. Anyone, at any moment, could come upon them and she would be ruined. Somehow, that knowledge only served to enhance the awareness careening through her.

Her nipples hardened, her breasts aching and full where they strained against him, and the strangest pulse of longing began between her thighs. Good heavens, he kissed as she would have supposed he would, with a masterful persuasion that marked him as a rake of the first order. She should not be so easily affected by a man with such dubious skill, and most definitely not by Warwick, of all men.

And yet, she was powerless to stop the desire that crashed over her as she shamelessly clambered closer to him. She had never wanted anything more than she wanted him.

He tore his mouth from hers and kissed a path of fire down her jaw to her ear. Pressing his lips to the sensitive shell, he whispered, "Do you believe I want to court you now?"

She shivered, tilting her head to allow him greater access to a part of her she had not previously supposed would be as desperate for Warwick's mouth as it was now. He obliged her, nuzzling her earlobe before running his tongue over the hollow directly behind it.

A moan escaped her before she could stifle it. Movement in the corner of her eye had her gaze flying to Jane, who had begun to stir. "Oh dear heavens," she hissed. "Warwick. Jane is waking. You must return to your seat."

"Damn," he cursed, pressing one more kiss to her neck before he hastily disengaged, stood, and stalked back to the chair upon which he had begun his call. Less than discreetly, he adjusted his breeches before seating himself once more.

Jane cleared her throat and shifted in her chair, adjusting her cap as she blinked sleep from her eyes. She did not appear to have witnessed a thing, thank heavens. Lydia took a deep, calming breath, hoping she didn't appear as thoroughly kissed and discombobulated as she felt.

"You did not answer," Warwick pressed, drawing her attention back to him once more. To his mouth, which had owned hers in a way she had not been able to imagine possible. "Do you believe me now, Lady Lydia?"

She swallowed, willing her heart to slow its frantic pace, and then surprised even herself when she said, "Perhaps I require further convincing, Warwick."

He grinned, and she felt that seductive smirk all the way to her toes. "Challenge gladly accepted."

CHAPTER 4

*A*n early snow had fallen, blanketing the landscape in white. While the snow was lovely to gaze upon, transforming the countryside with its tranquil beauty, Alistair appreciated the precipitation for a different reason entirely.

It gave him an excuse to drive about in a sleigh with Freckles.

Alone.

Seated side by side.

He handled the reins with expert ease, trying his best to stem the flow of heat that arrowed directly to his groin each time her soft body jostled his. It was a devilish form of torture to be so near to her and yet be unable to touch her.

In fact, it was bloody well hell.

Now that he had tasted her sweet, pink lips and run his tongue over her silken skin, his cock was having a difficult time understanding the finer points of propriety. *Mine*, railed the beast within him, longing to claim and conquer and take.

He could not blame it, for he was accustomed to taking what he wanted, when he wanted it. The ladies he had bedded in the past had not been ladies at all, nor had they been the sort who wore white dresses and required wooing. They had been demireps and wicked widows, the furthest one could get from prim innocence and virginal misses.

The furthest one could get from Freckles, and while his body didn't recognize the distinction, his mind did and was glad for it. He cast a glance in her direction, noting the stiff manner in which she held herself, staring straight ahead. Her profile was shaded beneath a bonnet trimmed by a spray of silk roses. Her hands were buried in a fur muffler, the blankets over her lap hiding much of her from view.

"You are quiet, Freckles," he observed at last, wondering what could so absorb her thoughts as to render her speechless. Unusual, that.

"The same could be said for you, Warwick." Her tone was tart, but she still did not face him, keeping her gaze trained anywhere but upon him.

"I was admiring the view." Although the words rolled fluently off his tongue, they were not empty flattery. He turned his eyes back to the vista ahead.

"The country looks the same today as it does every day after it has snowed," she clipped.

Intriguing. Freckles was not, nor had she ever been, a lady of brevity. What had her at sixes and sevens? Could it be that he was the source of her cool affectation—or, to be more apt, her reaction to him?

He found himself grinning. "That is decidedly not the view I spoke of."

When he threw another quick glance in her direction, her luscious lips had thinned into a straight, unwelcoming line. "You need not feel obliged to flatter me. There is nothing I dislike so much as insincerity."

"I am being nothing but sincere, Freckles." It was his turn to frown. "You insult me. Why would I flatter you?"

"I should think the answer as obvious as the reins in your hands." She paused. "You cannot even bring yourself to address me properly, and yet you claim to be entranced by my beauty, a beauty which no other man has ever been so affected by."

Ah. Her reaction to him was not what had her tied up in knots. Her pride was. Judging from yesterday's stringent litany of questions, she believed his interest in her to be caused by an ulterior motive. Her words returned to him.

It cannot be because of my dowry, can it?

Guilt stabbed through him at the reminder, banking the fires of lust raging in his veins. She was not entirely wrong in her assumptions, and he had neatly sidestepped her query by kissing her rather than answering. He should have told her the truth. Would have, had he not feared that in doing so she would reject him. Regardless of his pressing need for a wife with a substantial dowry, he wanted Freckles, and no other.

So, he had kissed her senseless, as much because he wanted to as because it helped his cause. He was more than aware he was a proficient kisser and that the ladies did not find fault with his face or form. If using that knowledge to his advantage made him a cad, then it couldn't be helped.

Her objections needled him, for they forced him to take a closer look at himself.

"Here, now." He cast her another, searching glance. "I have always called you Freckles. It is your sobriquet, is it not? And as for the rest, I merely said I was enjoying the view. I would never utter such folderol in the name of courting a lady."

She sent a furtive look in his direction at last, one delicate brow arched. "Folderol?"

His gaze met and held hers for a beat before he returned his attention to the horses. "I have not once, in all my years, told a lady I was entranced by her beauty. Nor would I."

He said the last with earnest conviction, for while he was no angel, neither was he a silver-tongued devil. It was not in his nature to ply his conquests with idle chatter. He far preferred deed over word. A cleverly placed kiss, a tender caress, the glide of his tongue over achingly sensitive, smooth female flesh.

Freckles had nearly come out of her skin when he had licked the hollow behind her ear, and he had fantasized all night about doing it again while he was planted deep inside her and she clenched around his cock. She had smelled of violets there, and something else that was distinctively feminine and purely hers. Decadent. Sweet.

Bloody mesmerizing.

"I am certain you have told many females a great deal of nonsense over the years, Warwick." Her arch tone pecked through his lust-hazed thoughts. "Whether or not you used those precise words is a moot point. The thing is…"

She trailed off, and he turned to her expectantly. "What is *the thing*, Freckles? Have out with it."

Her lips pursed as she seemed to muddle through what she wished to say. She looked adorably befuddled, and the driving desire to put his mouth on hers once more raged through him.

"The thing is, Your Grace," she began, "that you refer to me in the same manner with which one might speak about a butler, and you have known me for nearly my whole life, and I have always been a nuisance to you. I am more than aware that I am too tall and that I am rather more plump than convention considers appealing—"

"You have never been a nuisance, and neither are you plump," he intervened.

"That I am too opinionated," she continued as if he had not spoken at all, "that I am nearly on the shelf, and that you are a handsome and dashing duke to my spinster wallflower.

Yet suddenly, you declare yourself my suitor and follow me about this house party, daring to suggest that you are gazing upon me as if I am someone who would hold you in thrall when we both know quite well I am not."

He didn't know how to answer her concerns, for she was not precisely wrong that he had not always seen her as he did now. That was part of what he loved about the termagant. She was perceptive and observant, unafraid to embrace her intelligence and hoist it as a flag for all to see. But she was decidedly wrong about her not holding him in her thrall. Her artless loveliness hit him in the gut each time he looked at her.

"Would it help to know that I have also never kissed my butler?" he asked, attempting levity as a last recourse.

Freckles exhaled a disgusted sigh. "Have you gone mad, Warwick? Perhaps the strain of your father's death has been too much for you and you are now addle-brained. It is the only explanation for your developing this ludicrous notion that you wish to court me."

"Moreover," he continued as if she had not spoken, warming to his cause, "I never considered you a nuisance, not even when I rescued you, bedraggled and stinking of fish, from the pond that day."

"Stinking of fish!" Fury made her voice deep and husky.

He swallowed, shifting in his seat as his cock grew more rigid. What the hell was wrong with him that he could sit here arguing with her and yet think of nothing but touching her, kissing her, and making her his? Her anger was oddly lust-inspiring. Then again, this was Freckles, and everything about her was.

"You see?" Alistair gave her a heavy-lidded look. "I am honest to a fault. Obsequiousness has never been one of my sins."

"Oh." She huffed, her breath making a silver cloud in the

air, her bonnet stirring in her agitation. "You know what I mean, Warwick. Do not be obtuse. I know my faults, all of them, so do not expect me to believe you cannot spy every one for yourself."

"You are the perfect height," he countered, mentally ticking through her extensive arguments, "and your form is perfect, curved and pleasing and feminine just as it ought to be. You are intelligent, kindhearted, and quick-witted enough to flay any lesser opponent alive. If it has never occurred to you that I like you, Freckles, precisely for who and what you are, then you are a fool. You are precisely the sort of woman whom any man would be proud to take to wife."

"Any man." She made a dismissive sound. "Clearly that is not so."

"Perhaps not any man," he corrected gently, unable to keep himself from widening his legs so that his thigh pressed against hers through the layers of cloth and blankets separating them. She did not withdraw, and he wished he had a free hand to clasp hers or the privacy to kiss her once again, to taste her in all the places he longed to run his tongue. But they were not the only revelers about the Abingdon Hall park, and it would not do to court scandal.

"You see?" she chimed in, her tone exasperated. "Even you admit it."

"You are the sort of woman I would be proud to take to wife," he elaborated. "And I am heartily grateful no other has yet claimed you for his own, as that means you are mine."

She went silent. He risked another sidelong look in her direction. Freckles stared back at him, her brow furrowed. "You recently suffered a blow to the head. That is the only explanation. Are you with fever? Delirium is setting in? The cold weather has given you a lung infection."

He chuckled at her determination. "No, Freckles."

"You are serious." The last was a statement rather than a question.

"About making you my duchess?" He paused. "Utterly."

Another silence descended between them, and he swore he could hear the wheels of her agile mind turning.

"Why are you here at this house party?" she asked at length.

Of course, she would be curious, being the wily creature she was. Wise of her to note it was not the sort of thing he would have ordinarily done. "Why do you think?"

"You truly are searching for a wife, then?"

"No." A small smile flitted with the corners of his mouth. "I have already found her."

"Obsequiousness may not be one of your sins, but arrogance certainly is." She made a tsking sound. "I was right about you, Warwick. You are a rogue."

He did not miss the smile in her voice, and it filled his chest with something buoyant and unfamiliar and…warm.

By God, he rather liked it.

CHAPTER 5

"*T*oday will be a very fine one, Lydia," her mother chirped with the enthusiasm of a bird in spring.

But it was not spring. The snow on the ground and the chill in the air gave proof. Rather, it was the twenty-fifth of December.

Christmas.

And Lydia had been hiding from the festivities of the house party that afternoon, settled into a chair so she could read a book, when her mother had bustled into the small salon she had found, disrupting her solitude and quiet both. At least the house party was nearing its completion, and she could return to the familiar order of her ordinary life.

"Today seems no different than any other," she observed, frowning. "Aside from it being Christmas day."

"How wrong you are," Mother said. "It is a grand day for a celebration! The sun has appeared to melt the snow. I could turn into a watering pot, so great is my relief. But I shall not. No, indeed. I shall not."

Lydia glanced up from a volume of Newton's *Philosophiae Naturalis Principia Mathematica*. Her mother's white lace cap bobbed in her agitated excitement. Lydia blinked, slowly forcing herself to concentrate.

"Mother, are you quite well?" she asked, concern coloring her voice.

Her mother looked well enough, though she was perhaps more flushed than usual, twin flags of scarlet on her round cheeks. Her blue-gray eyes were unnaturally bright. With fever, perhaps? Lydia frowned, worry unfurling in her breast.

"I have never been so well, of that I can assure you. Oh, my darling girl, I despaired that you would forever remain unwed and on the shelf like your Aunt Clarinda." Mother clapped her hands in rather unladylike fashion, surprising when she was ordinarily such a stickler—no one in the world could muster even a pinch of Mother's deportment, aside from the dowager Duchess of Revelstoke. "But you have proven me wrong, and I could not be more proud. Such a feather in your cap! *The Duke of Warwick.* Imagine, you shall be a duchess. And all in time for Cecily to have her debut next Season."

Lydia blinked, allowing her mother's rapid staccato of exclamations to seep into her mind. Planetary motion was so much more intriguing than the marriage mart and house party games. She sifted through what her mother had said, attempting to resurrect the salient points. Aunt Clarinda. Something about a feather. The Duke of Warwick.

Ah, yes. *You shall be a duchess.*

Good heavens. Surely, she had heard her incorrectly. Mother had not just implied that she was to *wed* the *Duke of Warwick*...had she?

A gasp tore from her throat. "Mother, do you not think your celebration premature? He danced with me once and took me on a sleigh ride, aside from being about for all the festivities Lady Emilia planned."

Her mother's brow hiked to her hairline, nearly disappearing beneath her cap. "Of course he has proclaimed his interest, my dear. He has scarcely strayed from your side this last fortnight."

True. Warmth suffused her cheekbones as she recalled the recent whirlwind of activity that had unfolded in the wake of the enchanted day when he had taken her on a sleigh ride and insisted he would marry her. Empty flattery, she was sure of it. Warwick was a handsome devil, a rake of the first order. Not to be trusted. Certainly not the sort of man who would truly want her.

"He is friends with Rand," Lydia objected on principle. "I have known him nearly all of my life. We are guests at the same house party. Of course, he has been at my side."

"He has been courting you, my dear," Mother insisted, a pleased smile tempering the sometimes austere lines of her countenance. "No gentleman would dance attendance upon a lady or look upon a lady as he has you without intending to make an offer. He has not even looked twice at any of the Winter chits, thank the Lord."

Also true, Warwick always sought her out, danced with her, flirted with her. But he was Warwick. His nonsensical claims that he was courting her aside, the notion of him truly wishing to marry her was laughable. "I am sorry to disappoint you, Mother, but he does not care for me in such a manner."

Mother gawked at her, pressing a hand over her heart. "My darling girl, of course he does. Why do you think he is at this very moment speaking with your brother in the absence of Revelstoke?"

The air left Lydia's lungs. Warwick was meeting with Rand, and she had not known. Conducting an interview with him. It could only mean one thing. The very thing that her ridiculously thrilled mother had already ascertained.

Belatedly, she realized that her fingers were gripping the

Principia as though her life depended upon it. She inhaled slowly, attempting to calm herself, to stay the onslaught of worry beating to life within her. "Warwick is speaking with Rand?"

Her mother's head bobbed with more vigor than such a moment required. Her cap nearly went askew. "Of course, he is. Have you not been listening to a word I said, daughter? Oh, for shame. You and those cursed books. Do hide it somewhere, at the very least, Lydia, lest Warwick comes here and sees you with it in your lap. Revelstoke did you no favors in encouraging your unladylike pursuits during the course of your youth, I must confess."

Her mother's disgust for the leather-bound volume in Lydia's lap could not have been more pronounced had it been a dead fish instead of a book filled with valuable knowledge. Grandfather had been decidedly cut from different cloth than her mother, and Lydia would be grateful for that contrast every day of her life. Grandfather had encouraged her to pursue subjects and studies ordinarily *de trop* for a lady, much to her mother's shame.

"You wish me to hide my book?" she repeated the question to her mother, lest she had misheard or misunderstood.

Another bob of the bright-white cap. Lace fluttered. "Yes, and make haste. I expect he shall conclude his interview with Aylesford at any moment now."

Lydia absorbed the information her mother had just unceremoniously imparted. If she was to be believed, Warwick was currently meeting with Rand to formally ask permission to wed her. That meant he had been truthful that day in the sleigh. Truthful that night beneath the stars in the darkness of the Havenhurst garden. Honest when he had plied her with kisses in the parlor while Jane snored away.

That meant the Duke of Warwick wished to marry her. The beautiful, ridiculously rakish, always improper Duke of

Warwick wanted *her*, plump wallflower he had once fished from a pond.

Impossible. Improbable.

It was the sort of thing she wasn't even sure she would want.

What she most certainly did not want? To hide her reading proclivities from a man who would become her partner through life. She would sooner wrangle an elderly dowager's ill-behaved corgis than pretend to be someone she was not.

"Mother, the duke will either accept me as I am, if he truly wishes to wed me, or he will not." She shrugged. Also unladylike, but it could not be helped. "I will not hide my book from him."

Her mother's nose twitched, a sure sign that she was about to go into high dudgeon. "Put the thing away, Lydia. I beg you."

Lydia shook her head slowly. "No."

"Just when I thought you had finally procured some sense," Mother grumbled.

Her mother's insistence that Warwick was asking for her hand in marriage meant precious little if she could not have what she wanted most. Otherwise, she may as well become accustomed to the drudgery of life as a paid companion.

"I have sense," she felt compelled to argue. "And it is that very selfsame sense that refuses to allow me to hide a book from a man who would marry me as though it is a source of shame. I am not embarrassed by my mind, Mother, and neither should you be. I would sooner be on the shelf than sacrifice myself to a man who cannot see beyond the long end of his arrogant nose."

"I do hope you are not speaking of me, as I have it on good authority that my nose is neither arrogant nor overly long."

The lazy drawl emerging from the threshold of the room had Lydia's eyes flying to him. There he stood. Tall. Debonair. Appallingly handsome. He wore confidence better than his exquisitely tailored coat.

Warwick. He was *here*. Finished speaking with Rand. Pinning her beneath the full effect of that shockingly blue gaze. Making her forget for a moment that Mother had certainly erred and there was no way the divine, masculine creature before her would be interested in a gangly, shapeless lady who preferred the stars to the drawing room.

Mother gasped at his sudden, unexpected appearance. Lydia flushed, wondering how she had failed to notice his presence when every part of her now hummed into awareness at the sight of him. He performed a formal bow with glorious precision. Only his rakish air and the smug grin curving his lips hinted at his true nature. His smile deepened as he refused to remove his stare from her, and *oh dear heavens*. The mesmerizing twin grooves in his cheeks reappeared.

She and her startled mother exchanged perfunctory, perfectly polite greetings with him, Lydia's by force. That she could form a coherent sentence and feign a complete lack of concern at his presence were twin miracles.

"Of course, Lady Lydia was not speaking of you, Warwick." Her mother was quick to reassure him, either not sensing the inflection of humor in his words or not willing to risk the chance that he had found insult in Lydia's frank words.

"Very good," he murmured, not taking his eyes from Lydia. "I would hate to think Lady Lydia should find fault with me in any way."

No. How could anyone find fault with him when he was as dashing as any man she had ever seen? When he always knew precisely what to say? When a mere smile from his lips devastated her? She studied him as her mind whirred with the possibilities about to unfold.

Something new shone in his expression. His regard was almost intimate. Tender. It quite stole her breath even though she had no wish for it to affect her. How could she possibly gird her defenses against a man so fine-looking it nearly hurt to gaze upon him, who was everything a gentleman should be?

With dimples.

The dimples, simply, were not fair.

But when one stopped to consider the matter of the Duke of Warwick's appearance, neither was his face. Or the rich mahogany locks that begged to be smoothed by her palm. Never mind the sensual lips that knew how to kiss with such persuasion, lips she had felt against hers, plundering, claiming, taking. The reminder of that heated embrace was a spur in her wild thoughts. The heat in her cheeks heightened rather than abated, and yet she could not tear her gaze from him.

What had come over her? Who was this simpleminded miss who could not stop staring into the eyes of the Duke of Warwick? Who was imagining, for the very first time, that he might actually be hers?

That he might actually want *her*.

"Lady Lydia would never find any fault in you, Your Grace," Mother exclaimed then, winning Lydia's attention once more. Mother blinked, her smile clearly—at least to Lydia's well-trained eye—feigned. "Would you, my darling Lydia? Go on, tell him then."

Lydia blinked. "Mother, it was a figure of speech. You need not concern yourself on his account. Why, His Grace is well-versed in the art of jesting. He has been a *bon ami* to Rand, after all. I should hardly think it necessary to explain."

"You *were* speaking of me, then?" he asked with deceptive disinterest.

Her mother's eyes narrowed into a distinctive glare, mouth pursing into a knot. Lydia was sure that had Warwick not watched with such scrutiny, her mother would have mouthed her displeasure to her, or at the very least hissed a reprimand to be on her best behavior. Lydia looked back to Warwick. If she did not know better, she would venture to say he was unsure of himself.

But unsure and the Duke of Warwick were two components of the English language that could not comfortably dwell together in the same sentence. He was the most self-possessed, handsome man—and rake—she knew.

"Yes," she said with a smile of her own, enjoying the notion that she—who most other gentlemen had overlooked —might make him squirm.

"Of course, she was not," Mother interrupted with false gaiety. She made an exaggerated show of looking about her then, as though she had lost something quite dear and could not fathom where it had gone. "Good heavens, I seem to have misplaced my needlework. I must go off in search of it. I shall be back in a trice, and I shall leave the door ajar whilst I am away."

Lydia nearly groaned at her mother's blatant intention to leave her alone with Warwick. There had been no sign of needlework about. Not only did it go against the rigid strictures of propriety, but it left Lydia with a galloping pulse and a dry mouth as she watched her mother's skirts disappear over the threshold and realized she was well and truly alone with him.

Her gaze went to him now, studying. Appraising.

If he had indeed suffered a blow to the head, the effects did not seem destined for a reversal any time soon. Her eyes inventoried his lean frame. In his buff breeches and superfine jacket, with his pristine cravat and white waistcoat, he was the first stare of fashion. Every bit the Corinthian. So magnificent to look upon that she nearly ached. Yearning, unwanted and unexpected, tore through her.

There was no one to come between them as he stalked toward her with undeniable intent. They were alone in the cheerful little salon where her mother preferred to receive family and close friends. Not even her abigail Jane dozed nearby. There was no one. No one who could save her. No one who could keep her from acting the fool and succumbing to him.

She rose from her seat, prepared for flight.

He smiled knowingly at her perusal, his dimples making her heart thump fast against her breast once more. "Freckles."

She retreated from him as he advanced, until her back pressed against a wall and she had nowhere else to go. He flattened his palms against the cheerful wallcovering on either side of her head and pressed his sturdy frame against hers. For some reason, her eyes would not seem to move from his lips.

"Warwick," she said, for she, who had never been at a loss for words in her life, suddenly found she had nothing coherent to say.

His head bowed, until his mouth hovered a fraction from hers. "Your brother has given me permission to wed you in your father's stead, though I have also written Revelstoke, as a courtesy."

Her stomach bottomed out, much the way she expected it would had she been trapped inside a runaway carriage. A sharp, unexpected thrill mingled with shock and fear. It was true. The Duke of Warwick—the bold, self-assured rake pinning her in place with his large body and simmering presence—meant to marry her.

Meant to marry.

Her.

Lady Lydia Brownlow.

The words, like the realization, seemed to settle upon her haltingly. With them came the most ludicrous, pure burst of unadulterated joy. For a fleeting moment, the urge to press herself against him and turn her face up to receive his kisses soared through her.

Then, like any bird who had flown to impossible heights, she crashed to the Aubusson at her feet. No one had consulted her. Of course, Rand had not asked her if she desired such a match. Neither had Warwick. Mother had been deliriously happy at the prospect. They were all so very certain of her, and why would they not be?

It was a foregone conclusion that she, spinster and wall-flower with no other suitors who had come up to scratch, would marry a handsome duke. Heavens, it was a foregone conclusion she would wed *any* gentleman who asked for her hand.

How lowering.

She cocked her head, studying him. He was the most handsome man she had ever laid eyes upon, whilst she was commonplace as a sparrow. Why would he wish to marry her, when surely he had his pick of every diamond of the first water on the marriage mart? Lady Felicity, for instance, who was also in attendance.

"You wish to *marry me*? Me, Warwick?" If her tone was incredulous, it could not be helped, for her shocked mind spun in a deluge of questions, concerns, and disbelief.

"You," he agreed intently. His eyes bored into hers. At long last, his large hands settled upon her waist, finding it without err beneath the billowing muslin of her gown, his grasp possessive and not at all unwanted. "No one else will do."

He dipped his head then, his mouth seeking hers. She may have sighed into him, opening for the thrilling quest of his tongue. She may have run her tongue against his, tasting him, the spirits that he must have shared with her brother during their *tête-à-tête*. He was dark and decadent and everything she had never imagined she would want.

He kissed her with a slow languor that set fire to her from the inside. She felt flushed, aching, desperately in need of something she could not yet define. Something only he could give her. And she wanted it, how she wanted it. Wanted him.

But the logical part of her balked. That part of her had far too many questions that needed answers. She pulled her mouth from his with reluctance, staring up at him and noting that the dashing grin remained upon his lips. Lips that had kissed her. Soundly.

Looking upon him now, she rather felt like the child she had once been, gazing with longing at the most perfect apple on the tree. High over her head, the apple had been fiendishly out of reach. Now, it was as if the best apple on the tree had fallen into her lap. Hers to scoop up and savor.

With a swallow, she forced herself to find her composure. She was not ordinarily given to flights of fancy or romantic urgings. It was not her way. But this—Warwick—was changing everything. Kissing him was akin to looking into the night sky and seeing a new star for the first time, realizing that nothing was ever constant, that the universe was one of limitless possibilities.

The way he looked at her, the way he kissed her, she could almost believe this possibility was her new reality. But she would not capitulate so easily. "If you are to be believed," she said slowly, "you truly wish to marry me. Yet you have not yet asked *me* if I should like to wed you, Warwick."

His dimples disappeared, and she wished she could say their loss dampened the blinding effect of his masculine beauty, but the plain truth was that it did not. Nothing could diminish that tousled, mahogany hair, those slashing cheekbones and wonderfully formed lips, the flashing blue eyes, or his wide, angular jaw.

His right hand left her waist, and while she inwardly protested, he quickly mollified her as he trailed a finger down her cheek. Somehow, he had removed his gloves without her taking note, for his hand was bare. Skin met skin. Warmed and tingled wherever the firm pad of that long finger touched.

"You did not yet give me the opportunity, my dear, and I shall remedy it now." His finger stroked down her jaw to her throat, leaving a trail of fire. "I have never met another lady whom I admire more. You are intelligent, capable, and lovely, and all that is kind and good, despite your propensity for referring to me as a sapskull."

He won a laugh from her, the rogue. "You *are* a sapskull, Warwick."

But his words had warmed her in a place she hadn't known existed, deep inside. Could it be true that he admired her mind and that he thought her lovely even when she knew she was not? Or was it merely false flattery from a man who had a whispered string of conquests numbering in the dozens?

"I am," he agreed, his expression serious, and so intent that it seemed to pierce her. "I will be the first to admit that I do not deserve a lady of your immeasurable worth. And yet, I find I am horridly selfish. Even should I search to the ends of the realm, I would not find anyone more suited to me than you. Will you be my wife, Lady Lydia Brownlow?"

As he asked the question, he opened his hand directly over her heart, soaking in its frantic beats. Lydia searched his gaze, struggling to sift through thoughts muddied by his nearness and his touch, by her body's overzealous reaction to him. Did he truly mean those words, or were they meaningless flattery, easily spoken from his silver tongue?

"I do not…that is to say…" Her words trailed away as she struggled to make sense of it all. "Warwick, you cannot be serious about this. I have never been aught but a nuisance to you, trailing after you and Rand where I was not wanted. Why, we do not even get on, you and I."

He shook his head slowly, his eyes dipping to her lips. "Never a nuisance, Freckles. As for getting on, need I remind you of all the time we have enjoyed together at this house party?"

No. She did not require assistance in recalling his searing kisses or smoldering glances, or the way it felt to be held in his arms. The rightness of it all, in spite of herself. The yearning he had brought to life in her foolish heart.

She frowned. "You are well-versed in the art of kissing, Warwick. Such is the way of things with all rakes, I imagine."

He leaned nearer, his mouth almost upon hers once more. "Who said anything about kissing, Freckles?"

She flushed, forcing herself to ignore the delightful way his body pressed into hers, the rich scent of him, pleasant and inviting, the breadth of his shoulders in his coat. Above all, she would not be affected by the wicked dimples that had chosen that moment to once again reveal themselves as he smiled.

"You are a scourge," she muttered. "I cannot think why my brother would consider your offer for my hand."

But of course, she could. They both could. Rand was his friend. Warwick was a duke, and Lydia was on her last season before retiring firmly to the shelf. He very wisely refrained from pointing that out.

"Perhaps he thinks, as I do, that we would suit immensely. I want to gaze up at the night sky with you, to waltz with you, to make you laugh. I want you to be my duchess, to bear me children, to walk through this life with me." His tone was earnest. He pressed a kiss to the corner of her mouth. "Lydia, sweet. Tell me you will be mine. I want to begin the new year with you as my bride."

I want to gaze up at the night sky with you.

Perhaps it was that single phrase. Perhaps it was the passion of his gaze burning into hers. Mayhap it was even the slow seduction of his wonderful mouth so near to hers, hovering at the corners, settling over her bottom lip, teasing and tasting. Or his tongue, swiping the seam, slipping inside to taste her. His hand, sliding beneath her heart to cup her breast through her gown. His body, crowding her into the wall until there was no escape, and all she could see, feel, and breathe was him.

And it still wasn't enough.

She wanted more.

She wanted everything he spoke of. Most of all, she simply wanted the Duke of Warwick, with a ferocity that scared the wits out of her. She could not—would not—turn him away now, but neither would she simply acquiesce. "I will agree to be your wife, Warwick, but I do have requirements."

"Requirements," he repeated, as though she had said she would like to venture to the moon.

"Yes." She warmed to her cause, knowing that while she would have precious few rights as a married lady, Warwick was a gentleman. While he was undeniably a rake, he still possessed scruples. She had seen his kindness, gentleness, goodness, and honor. If she asked him to honor her wishes, she had to believe that he would. As things stood, her options were to either marry Warwick—the devil she knew—one of her other suitors, or to become a companion. She chose Warwick, just as he had chosen her.

"These…requirements, Freckles. What can they be?" His brow furrowed, and he seemed less imposing in his vexation.

Lydia smiled, sensing she had already won this particular battle. "First is fidelity, Warwick. I do not wish to marry a gentleman who will keep a…"

"Mistress." His dimples returned, diminishing her defenses once more. "You have my word that I do not currently have one, nor will I take one, as you are all that I desire."

His words sent a fresh surge of heat and yearning through her, but she tamped it down. Could it be that he desired her? That the Duke of Warwick, handsome, self-assured Corinthian, desired a plain, plump spinster who preferred burying her nose in a book to dancing at a ball?

Silver tongue, she reminded herself. *He is a rogue.*

Still, he seemed genuine. She forced herself to forge onward before she lost her nerve. "Second: you will agree not to become an impediment in my thirst for knowledge."

"Gads no," he was quick to respond. "I admire your sharp mind, Freckles. I do not seek to bury it."

Excellent. "If I wish to read a book that is not considered suitable material for a lady, you will not object."

His grin widened, showing twin rows of even, white teeth. "What sort of book have you in mind, love? I may have a tome or two that you would find of interest."

Of course, he did, the knave. How was it that he could charm her with his raffish ways? Nor did she overlook that particular term of endearment that had rolled so fluently off his tongue. *Love.*

Oh, heavens. Why was it so blessedly stuffy in the chamber all of a sudden? And why was he looking upon her with expectation, as though he awaited her next words? Belatedly, it occurred to her that she was meant to be setting up the foundation for their union, not gazing at him with witless adoration.

Adoration? Who was she, and where had the real Brownlow gone? Drat. Had she just thought of herself as Warwick's pet name for her? Indeed, she had. Obviously, she was a hopeless cause.

Think, Lydia. What other concessions would you have him make?

"If I am to marry, I would hope that my husband could be my friend. That we would look after each other. Help each other. Respect each other." She paused, thinking of the sort of marriages common to the *ton*, the sort she did not wish for herself. "If you cannot meet these requirements, tell me now. I would sooner be a companion than accept anything less."

"Freckles."

The way he said her name answered a hunger deep within her.

She could not look away from that burning gaze. "Yes?"

"I agree to each one of your demands, my lady pirate." He paused, a wicked grin curving his lips. "Now, will you consent to be my duchess?"

The time had come to make her choice, and it was not at all how she had imagined it would be. For she knew instinctively that a marriage with Warwick would be unlike anything she was prepared for. He was sensual and dangerous, and so very different from her other suitors, who seemed somehow bland and tepid in comparison. Her other suitors were the safe perch atop a hill in the midst of flood waters. Warwick was the flood.

But something within her whispered that he was *her* flood. And she wanted to be swept away for once in her life. To take a risk. To leave caution and fear behind her, moving forward into the unknown. She looked at Warwick now, really looked at him, and she longed to be reckless. Full stop.

With a deep, calming breath, Lydia tipped up her chin and answered. "I will."

She had no time to rethink the wisdom of her acceptance. His mouth pressed to hers at last, and it was as if he kissed her for the first time, tender and masterful, a gentle claiming, and she thought then that if she wasn't careful, she could fall in love with him. His tongue traced the seam of her lips, sweeping inside to taste her. Someone made a sound of yearning. Her? Him? She wasn't sure. She clutched his broad shoulders; he cupped her breast. Her nipple pebbled into his palm.

More was all she could think as she sucked his tongue, swallowed his taste, committed the sensation of his solid body beneath her eager fingers to memory. More was what she wanted. Needed. How and when had he become precisely what she longed for?

They broke apart for a breath, and it was then that Mother returned, noisily thumping into the door so that it landed with a dull thud against the wall. Lydia turned away from Warwick, breathless, hoping her mother had not seen their embrace.

Mother smiled, holding the embroidery she had been working on for the last month aloft. "My needlework has been found, and just in time, I should think."

Lydia's cheeks burned. Well, then. How mortifying, but all told, she rather liked being referred to as a lady pirate. Indeed, it was a mantle she would wear with pride.

"Merry Christmas, Freckles," Warwick murmured to her.

"Merry Christmas," she whispered back.

Perhaps Mother had been right about the day after all.

CHAPTER 6

ONE MONTH LATER

*N*othing could have prepared Alistair for the moment when he crossed over the threshold separating his chamber from the duchess's quarters and saw Freckles for the first time.

His wife.

Breathtaking perfection.

She wore a demure white *robe de chambre* adorned in lace, belted loosely at her narrow waist. Her lovely auburn curls—coiled in an elaborate affair for their wedding ceremony earlier that day in St. George's—was unbound and hung down to her waist in striking contrast against the light fabric. Her feet were bare, her nicely turned ankles barely visible beneath the hem. Her face was pale, arresting. He could not stop staring at that full, pink mouth. Those gray-blue-flecked eyes, her elegant cheekbones, the delicate arches of her brows.

His mouth went dry.

He stopped where he was, drinking in the sight of her, and a realization hit him with the force of a rampaging stallion, straight in the chest. The odd sensation that rushed through him whenever he was in her presence, the anticipation from the moment he left her side until he could be back again. The pounding of his pulse, the restless need to be with her, to have her in his bed, to make her his once and for all... the reason no other lady would do as the Duchess of Warwick...everything made sense. It was as if someone had lit a lamp in a dark cellar and he could now see with perfect vision.

He *loved* her. He loved Freckles.

Damn and blast. He could not move. Could not think. She was his at last, standing nervously before him in her wedding night finery, his to touch, his to kiss.

His to take to bed.

Nothing had ever seemed so right, and yet he remained trapped. Rooted to the Aubusson in wizened old oak tree fashion, brain wildly fumbling to make sense of what he felt and what he knew. Could it be true? Did he truly love her? He, who had not ever imagined he possessed the capability for such an emotion? He, who had always rather imagined love to be the sort of rot more suited for plays and operas than real life?

That strange sensation whenever he thought of Freckles? The way he could not get enough of her scent, or how the sound of her voice thrilled him to his bloody toes? Or how he longed to kiss her every time he saw her, the utter torture he had suffered these last two months in waiting for this very moment, this precise night, when he could at last make her his. As she ought to be. In every way.

Why, then, could he not move?

"Husband," she greeted hesitantly into the awkward silence he had created by lingering at the threshold like a lumbering oaf.

One word from her, and his cock went rigid.

Ridiculous though it was, she seemed more composed

than he, a seasoned rake who had charmed more than his fair share of females in his day. "Freckles," he returned, his throat thick with unspoken emotion and pent-up need. Good God, what if she didn't love him?

She fidgeted with the ends of her lustrous hair, the only sign that she was at all discomfited, and that only because he knew her well. Her luscious pink lips formed a smile, and he wanted to feel it beneath his mouth. "Will you not call me Lydia now that we are wed, Warwick?"

She had always been Freckles to him, from the moment she had been a spirited little hoyden running wild up until now, when he understood that Freckles would no longer do. That chapter of their life had closed. She was his duchess now.

She was Lydia.

His love.

He cleared his throat, feeling as if he were hopelessly adrift in a boat on the ocean that he had only just learned was taking on water. But he would have to do something, would he not? Say something, certainly. She gazed upon him expectantly, her beauty almost ethereal in the chamber's soft light.

"Lydia," he said simply before thinking better of it and trying again. "Lydia, my love."

Her eyebrows arched at the endearment, and he wondered for a brief, breath-stealing beat whether she would ever return his feelings. She had not agreed to this union with the keen enthusiasm one might have expected of a blue-stocking facing a future as a companion to a cantankerous old curmudgeon. He had gone to Oxfordshire to spend Christmas with her, followed her about like an obedient pup, and she had still rattled off a list of requirements before reluctantly pledging her troth.

He did not begrudge her the requirements, for they were

reasonable and every bit of it was quintessentially Freckles, but he rather fancied she could have been a trifle more thrilled at the prospect of marrying him. He was considered a good catch, after all, and neither his face nor his form had ever met with feminine disapproval. Quite the opposite, in fact. More than anything, he wanted, with a ferocity that shook him, for her to love him back.

Sweet Christ, he was besotted.

"May I call you Alistair?" she asked, her voice hesitant.

She sounded so unlike her ordinary, authoritative self that it was enough to nudge him at last from his impromptu vigil on the threshold. His hands itched to hold her, to acquaint themselves with her lithe curves and learn her every dip and swell. In just a few strides, he stood before her, the tempting scent of violets teasing his senses. With Herculean effort, he checked the urge to take her in his arms and throw her to the bed before ravishing her senseless.

Lydia was not one of his usual conquests. She was innocent and perfect, and unlike every other woman he had bedded before her, she mattered to him in a way that humbled him to his very toes. He drew an arm around her, pressing his palm to the gentle curve of her spine just before the flare of her bottom. With his other hand, he traced a featherlight touch over her cheekbone, savoring the silken smoothness of her skin.

"Yes," he murmured, falling into her riveting gray eyes. "Call me Alistair, my love."

He could not wait to hear his name on her lips as he drove home inside her. Another surge of hot, all-consuming lust swept over him. He had never wanted a woman so much, and the force of his need shook him, making his hand tremor as he trailed a caress down her petal-soft throat before he buried his fingers in the waterfall of tresses at her nape.

"Alistair," she breathed, pressing her palms to his shoulders and stepping into his body so that the hardened peaks of her lush breasts grazed his chest.

Damn. He grew even harder. "Say it again," he commanded, angling her head back so that he could devour her mouth as he wished.

"Alistair."

His lips met hers in the next instant. He meant to kiss her tenderly, but when she opened for him, her tongue darting out to meet his, he could not control himself a moment longer. He kissed her with every last drop of passion raging through him, with all the love, the reverence. She made a sound in her throat, a whimper of desire, and it inflamed him more. Their tongues writhed together, mouths open and hungry. Her fingers sank into his hair, twisting, holding him to her as she kissed him back with just as much abandon.

She caught his lower lip between her teeth and nipped, tearing a strangled moan from him. Damn it, he had not anticipated her boldness, and it was enough to make his ballocks ache with a deep need for release. Of course, he ought not to be surprised. How like Lydia to be as fierce a lover as she was a person, unapologetic and fearless.

He broke the kiss and caught her up in his arms without a moment's hesitation, carrying her to the freshly turned-out bed dominating the far wall. The day had been onerous and rife with duty—the ceremony, the wedding breakfast, welcoming her to his household and performing introductions, a polite dinner as husband and wife—but now, at last, it was time to take what was his.

"Alistair," she protested as he made his way across the chamber. "I am too tall and ungainly to be carried about. I insist you put me down at once."

"Your servant, Duchess." With a wicked grin, he dropped her into the center of the bed.

She laughed, her gray eyes dancing, mouth red and

swollen from his kiss. Her smile was something to behold, for it didn't merely enhance her beauty. It made her somehow…luminous. "Perhaps you ought to take care in your proclamations, lest I force you to honor them."

He wore nothing beneath his dressing gown. Originally, he had thought not to offend her maidenly sensibilities by completely disrobing before her their first night. But now he could see the wrongness of it. She was his Lydia, and she had bitten his lip as if it were a sweet. He wanted every drop of uninhibited wickedness she had to give.

"I assure you that I did not misspeak." His fingers went to the belt keeping his dressing gown in place. "Indeed, I would like nothing more than to be your servant, my love."

Her eyes rounded as she took in his meaning. When he undid the knot and shucked the robe altogether, standing before her naked, her eyes went even wider. Her gaze traveled the length of him, lingering on his erect cock, and her tongue darted out to wet her lips. A charming flush crept over her cheekbones, down along the regal column of her throat, and disappeared beneath her *robe de chambre*. He wondered where it stopped.

Slow and precise in his movements, he joined her on the bed, kneeling at her dainty feet. He grasped her slim ankles, relishing the brand of her warmth entering his palms and radiating throughout his body with a poignant hum of pure, molten need.

All traces of levity were gone from her face as he met her shocked stare. "Warwick, what in heaven's name do you think you are doing? Studying my feet? I insist you cease at once."

His grin deepened. She was the oddest female, and he loved her for it. No other lady had ever dared to order him about in the bedchamber. He ran his thumbs over the knobby bone of each ankle. Slowly, he pulled them to opposite sides of the bed, opening her legs. She still wore her dressing gown over a chemise, maintaining her modesty, and the sight of her lying on the bed, covered in white linen and lace, thighs slowly parting, nearly undid him.

"Your feet are beautiful," he told her, lowering his head to drop a kiss to the top of first the left, then the right. His hands, meanwhile, continued their westward and eastward journey, opening her legs even wider.

"Warwick," she protested again. "You bedlamite, my feet are disproportionately large for a lady. No one in his right mind would think them beautiful." She wriggled then, shimmying her bottom in an effort to shake free of his hold. Instead of liberating herself, however, she only served to send the hem of her robe and chemise upward, over her knees.

Good Lord, another shimmy would send it over her thighs. "Stubble it, wife. Your feet are as perfect as the rest of you."

He kissed her ankles next, his starving gaze taking in the sight of her calves and kneecaps. He had never once been entranced by the sight of a lady's knees before tonight. But he could not help himself. Like a supplicant, he kissed his way up her legs, running his tongue in the hollow behind each knee where he discovered she was particularly sensitive.

"Good heavens, Warwick." His name was a moan.

He licked again. Kissed. Raked her sensitive flesh with his teeth before glancing up her body and meeting her gaze. "Alistair, my love. Else you shall once again be Freckles."

"I am sure I do not even know who I am at the moment," she said, her busy hands finding his hair once more. "Oh, good heavens."

"Yes," he agreed darkly, pushing the hems of her nightwear higher, until they reached the tops of her thighs. He urged her knees apart, and dropped a kiss to each inner thigh.

"Alistair," she gasped, and it was adorable. "This is depraved. You must not."

He smiled, the heat and musky scent of her near and tempting. Her tone and her body's response to him both told him that she wanted this every bit as much as he did. But she liked control, and venturing into the unknown surely had her at sixes and sevens. "I must."

He kissed higher, stroking her thighs. She was perfect, so bloody perfect, and he could only thank God that none of her other suitors had ever recognized the gem before them. That she had somehow, by some stroke of magic, become his.

He went higher still, to the enticing curves of her hips, so near to her center that her flesh, glistening and pink and so damn enticing, was visible. Just a tongue's stroke away. He glanced back up at her, that beautiful face at the end of the white fabric, and he wished she was naked so that he could admire the rise and fall of her breasts, the dip of her belly, so that he could see her as she was meant to be seen. "I want to taste you, love. Will you let me?"

Her lips fell open. He had shocked her, and though he knew he should be ashamed, he could not regret—not even for an instant—giving in to how very much he wanted her. All of her.

"Alistair?" Uncertainty underscored her voice.

He blew air over her seam, gratified by the answering, swift buck of her hips. "Do you trust me, my love?"

She didn't hesitate in her answer. "Yes."

He was humbled. Gratified. And he was going to bloody well worship this woman. This woman he loved. His wife.

His.

Something primal overcame him. He dragged his hands to her bottom, cupping her arse, and lifted her to his mouth.

He licked into her, closed his lips over her responsive pearl, sucked, worked it with his teeth. She tasted like the abundance of spring, like sweetness and musk, salt and sea, earth and life and everything that was necessary. Nothing had ever tasted so bloody good on his tongue, and he knew instinctively that nothing ever would.

Listening to her sounds, following the cues of her body, he learned her. Found what she liked. Just where she liked his tongue, how firmly she wanted his teeth to rake that sensitive bundle of flesh. He didn't stop until he had her where he wanted her, and she shook and spent against him, crying out in a soft exhalation, her body tremoring, coating his tongue with her essence.

And then, he rose on his haunches, dragged her robe and chemise the rest of the way up her body. He didn't stop undoing and tugging until all of it was gone, and he knelt between her thighs, admiring the pale gloriousness of her form in all its splendor.

"Lydia." Her name became a caress as he ran his hands up her long legs to her waist, and then higher still. He cupped the firm, round globes of her breasts, thumbed her hard nipples. "Lydia, my darling."

"Please," she cried out, writhing beneath him, her slick folds undulating against his aching cock.

Breath hissed from his throat, and he knew he would not last much longer. Bowing his head, he sucked a nipple into his mouth. He licked and nipped, kissing along the ridge of her collarbone, her neck, the spot behind her ear that made her wild. "I want inside you, love."

"Yes." She gasped when the head of his shaft grazed her pearl with each movement of her hips against him. Her hands traveled over his body, fanning flames of desire into a raging inferno. Over his chest, his arms, his back. Tentative strokes that gave way to bold strokes. "Alistair, I cannot wait."

He kissed her then, instead of answering, a long, deep claiming, allowing her to taste herself on his lips. She was sweet, so bloody sweet. Everywhere. He guided himself to her entrance, breaking his mouth away for a moment to gaze down at her. God, she was lovely, her hair a dark halo about her face, her blue-flecked eyes glazed with passion. His wallflower bluestocking turned to fire in his arms.

"There will be pain," he rasped, poised to take her. So bloody close to heaven. "I will go slowly, my love."

She nodded. "I trust you, Alistair."

The simple statement sent a stab of guilt straight into his gut. She did trust him—he could see her open heart and innocence there in her sparkling gaze. He did not deserve her trust, for he had not been truthful with her about his need for her dowry. It nettled him now, with a fierce persistence, but the damage had already been done. He would tell her, he promised himself, as soon as he could. Nothing could induce him to ruin this night, this chance to make her his.

He kissed her again, and thrust his hips, sheathing just the tip of himself within her tight, wet channel. She gasped against his lips, and though it nearly killed him, he remained still, allowing her to adjust before he proceeded.

"All right, love?" he asked.

She kissed him lingeringly. "All right."

Their mouths clung. He slipped a hand between their bodies where they were joined, delving into her slick folds to tease her where he knew she liked. Another slow roll of his hips, and the last barrier between them was broken. She stiffened beneath him, fingernails biting into his shoulders, but never ended the kiss, her tongue sliding into his mouth in a mimicry of the way he thrust inside her. And then she moved beneath him, bringing him deeper.

He kissed the corner of her mouth.

"Alistair," she murmured, clenching around his cock. "I will not break."

No, she would not. His wife was strong and capable, and at her urging, he canted his hips, fully seating himself. She released a seductive sigh, beginning to move with him. As one, they went together, over the edge of passion, reaching heights he hadn't even known existed. She was perfection. He thrust. Everything he had imagined and more. Another pump. Fingers worked over her flesh, bringing her to a frenzy until she tightened and shuddered on him, spending again. Another thrust. He was keenly aware of every sensation: the sounds of their bodies meeting, the scent of violet and arousal perfuming the air, the sweet taste of her on his tongue, her breasts crushed against his chest, nails raking skin, her long legs around his waist, her mouth urging him on.

One more swivel of his hips and he buried himself inside her to the hilt, losing himself, filling her with his seed. He rocked into her again and again as the waves crashed over him, and he found himself in her.

"Lydia," he whispered against her lips. He had not told her the full truth, but on this night, he would tell her the only truth that mattered. "I love you."

CHAPTER 7

*T*he next fortnight proved the happiest, most charmed of Lydia's life. She and Alistair enjoyed a honeymoon at his townhouse, and while it was not the ordinary way of things for a newly married couple, she could find no fault in it. They were not at home to anyone. No social calls, no visitors, no balls or soirees as the Season had yet to begin. Instead, they spent their days talking, laughing, and making love.

Love, Lydia thought with a secretive smile as she put the finishing touches on her toilette for dinner that night. She wore her hair in a loose fashion, piled at her crown with curls framing her face, a simple evening gown of claret red, her bosom on display for her husband's benefit. He possessed an equal fondness for her bosom, her legs, her hair, and her wit. Of the four, Lydia had only ever been proud of the last. Her bosom was too small, her legs too long, and her hair a dull, uninspiring shade of not-quite-red and not-quite-brown.

Her husband had informed her that her bosom was perfection, her legs drove him mad, and her hair was the most bewitching shade of auburn. None of it was, as her cynical inner scientist initially suspected, rooted in meaningless flattery. No, Alistair actually loved the very parts of her she had always detested most. He made her feel wanted, desirable, and beautiful… He made her feel the same coursing joy that she felt when she gazed upon the night sky and marveled at its brilliance and its endless, innate secrets. He made her feel powerful and awestruck all at once.

She had not imagined it possible for another person to complete her. Indeed, before their marriage, she had not realized she was half in need of a whole, even if she could so clearly see now that Alistair—*love*—was precisely what she had been lacking. It still thrilled her to think of his confession the night of their wedding.

Love was an emotion she had never expected to succumb to, and it was certainly the last thing she had expected from the Duke of Warwick. Yet, he surprised her almost daily as he revealed all the facets of himself.

With a deep, steadying breath, Lydia gave her reflection one last survey in the glass before heading down to dinner. Tonight was to be a night of firsts. Not only was it the first night that she and Alistair would officially welcome guests to their home as a married couple, but it was also the first night that she would tell him that she loved him too.

She had been too scared to say the words before now, too uncertain if what she felt for him was even real. Infatuation, after all, was one thing when it came to a gentleman of his impeccable looks. Love, however, seemed altogether foreign for a pragmatic soul like herself.

But time—and Alistair—could change everything.

And she was desperately, hopelessly in love with her husband. She just hoped that he would accept the gift of her heart and treat it with tender care.

༄

For the first time in a fortnight, Alistair had been forced to share his wife, and though it had been with family, that didn't render the obvious signaling of their honeymoon's end any more palatable. He had to admit that not having her to himself rather left him feeling out of sorts, like a bear who'd been unceremoniously rousted from hibernation.

Of course, he knew that all good things must necessarily conclude, as in one's glorious post-nuptial phase, which had been a series of laughing, loving, kissing, bedding, and occasionally pausing for sustenance. But logic had no place in his mind these days, at least not when it came to Lydia.

So he suffered through a stilted session of obligatory port with his father-in-law and Rand following dinner, the glare and brooding silence his friend continued to direct his way rather disconcerting. Rand had been well-pleased with his marriage to Lydia. But since his own nuptials had occurred not long thereafter, Alistair had seen precious little of his friend.

"My daughter seems quite happy, Warwick," Revelstoke said suddenly into the quiet before puffing on a cigar. "I am well pleased the two of you wed at last."

"It is my fondest wish to make her the happiest woman alive," he said, for it was the truth.

"Utter rot," Rand growled, finally breaking his silence. "You're a heartless bastard who took advantage of a bluestocking who was on the shelf. Do not pretend to have a care for my sister's happiness."

Alistair stiffened, eying his sometime friend. Surely, he had not just so openly dishonored him? "I beg your pardon?"

Rand refused to look away or abandon his cause. Instead, he stared Alistair down. "Have not your debts all been paid?"

He had discovered the truth.

Guilt hit him like a fist to the gut.

"They were my father's debts," he gritted.

"The sins of the father," Rand sneered. "You did not answer my question. Did you not use my sister's dowry to settle the damn debts? Did you truly think I would never uncover the truth?"

Of course, he had, for it had either been that or face losing all, even if doing so had left him feeling sick. The time had come for him to confide in Lydia about his father's debts, and he knew it.

Her generous dowry had settled all with plenty to spare, meaning he could begin rebuilding his estates. He should have told her before now, and he recognized his error with a twist in his gut. Part of him had been too selfish to mar their bliss with such a heavy revelation, but part of him was terrified to jeopardize the relationship blossoming between them by revealing the truth.

He clenched his jaw, forced himself to answer, "Yes, I used a portion of the dowry to settle my father's debts, but if you dare to suggest that my intentions toward my wife are anything other than pure, you may as well name your second."

"Aylesford," Revelstoke bit out, using Rand's courtesy title in a sure sign of displeasure. "Warwick. You will both cease posturing. Though you may be men grown, I am older and wiser, and believe me when I assure you no good will come of further such discourse this evening. Let us return to the ladies so we can once more recall that we are gentlemen."

Grimly, Alistair stood. "Yes, let us rejoin the ladies before any graver errors are committed here."

He stalked from the chamber, the fury filling him as much for himself as for Rand. After all, he could not say he would act or think any differently were he in his friend's boots. He knew as well, his conscience needling him with increasing persistence, that he should have been honest with Lydia and with Rand from the beginning. That he should have told them both about the debts and his need of a dowry. He would have done so had he not feared that it would ruin any chance he'd ever possessed of making her his duchess.

Losing Lydia was not something he could have withstood.

So, he had remained silent. Had swallowed his self-loathing. Had married her, made love to her, shared the happiest moments of his entire bloody life with her. All whilst he had been living a lie.

It was shameful.

His gaze lit on her when he entered the drawing room. God, she was beautiful, and the mere sight of her left his chest feeling simultaneously full and hollow, as if she gave him everything yet had the uncanny power to take it all away. She sat calmly amongst her mother, Rand's wife, and her younger sister. Lady Cecily was currently putting her pianoforte skills to good use. The chit was skilled and lovely, and Alistair had no doubt she would find a match easily enough, if one were the sort of gentleman who enjoyed such trivialities.

He far preferred an auburn-haired siren with a sharp mind, long legs, perfect curves, and a mouth that was temptation incarnate. The sort of lady who wasn't afraid to speak her mind or berate a duke, a lady who stared into the heavens with wonder yet could name each constellation. His wife. The woman he loved. The very woman he would tell the truth to tonight when they were alone. He could only hope she would find it in her heart to understand and forgive him.

And maybe, if he were truly fortunate, one day love him as much as he loved her.

She bestowed a pleased smile of welcoming upon him

that made him feel as though he were the only one present in the room. He grinned back at her like the lovesick fool he was, and took his place at her side, catching her hand and bringing it to his lips for a kiss. Violets hung in the air. He wanted to kiss her so much he nearly did right there before her entire family. With great effort, he held himself in check.

"Darling," he whispered so that only she could hear, "I missed you."

She giggled and gave him a good-natured swat. "Silver-tongued scoundrel," she murmured without heat. "We were separated for a mere half hour, no more."

"The longest half hour of my life."

A smile played about her lips. "Behave."

Duly chastised, he listened to Lady Cecily play. After an eternity passed, she stood to applause, none more rigorous than that emerging from the Duchess of Revelstoke, who was clearly a proud mama.

"That was lovely, Cecily," her grace said with a sniff. "Was it not, Rand? Be a good brother and tell her how well she plays so she may have the confidence to play in larger gatherings. Nothing will win a husband as surely as your gift with the pianoforte, my dear."

Warwick stifled a snort. He rather begged to differ on that assertion, but as he was not the appropriate audience for Lady Cecily's skills, it was a moot point. Alistair looked to Rand, who was not looking in his youngest sister's direction. Instead, he pinned Alistair with the glare of a predator sizing up his prey, determining the appropriate time to strike.

Bloody hell.

He knew his friend all too well, and what was about to happen could not be good. "Yes, Aylesford," he goaded, for if anyone was to strike first, it would be he. "Be a good brother."

"A good brother, you say?" Rand cocked his head,

pretending to consider Alistair's words as the rest of the company gazed on in alarmed confusion. "Ah, yes. But I am not one, am I? If I had been, Lydia would not be wed to your sorry hide right now. Would she, Warwick? I should have seen through your lies and uncovered what I now know before your nuptials. Now it is too late, but I can still right the wrongs you've done her."

He felt Lydia's gaze on him, sensed the questions and tension rising within her. But they had come too far to stop now. Dread, cold and sickly, unfurled within him. His hands felt like ice, his face frozen, his heart pounding.

"What lies are you speaking about?" he asked quietly.

"Aylesford," Revelstoke interjected.

"Good heavens, Rand," huffed the duchess simultaneously, sounding ruffled. "What can you be about? Do cease this nonsense at once."

"Aylesford," cautioned his wife, her countenance growing worried.

"I have discovered," Rand said slowly, his gaze going to Lydia, "that you were indebted up to your eyebrows. That your father owed nearly all he had to the cent-per-centers, and only a handsome dowry would rescue you from utter penury. All of that would be the truth, would it not, Warwick?"

"It would," he agreed tightly. There it was, then, sparing him the duty of confessing himself. "Shall I thank you now or later, Aylesford?"

"Alistair."

He turned at the tortured, almost pleading note in Lydia's voice, and faced her. "Lydia, love. I can explain," he said quietly, hoping she would wait. Would allow him to speak to her without an audience, reveal everything and let her cast her judgment as she saw fit.

She searched his gaze, the happy flush leaching from her

skin and leaving her a pale husk of the bold beauty he could not wrest his eyes from all evening long. The transformation cut him with the precision of an assassin's blade, deep and true, finding its mark.

"Is it true?" she demanded, a tremor in her voice that even she—redoubtable as she was—could not suppress.

He would not prevaricate, as it would do him more harm than good. But how could he feign protest, offer glib reassurances, when she looked at him as if he had crushed the very heart of her beneath his boot heel?

"Yes," he admitted, his jaw tightening so much that pain radiated through his teeth. It was not enough penance. No amount of suffering on his behalf would be. How could he rectify the isolation he saw in her expression, the pain?

The loathing?

"My God." Her nostrils flared, her hand going to her mouth as though she were about to be ill.

The enormity of her reaction hit him with the force of a blow straight to his chest. He nearly doubled over from the magnitude of it. "Lydia, please." He caught her hand in his, squeezing her unresponsive fingers. "Let us speak alone after our guests have gone. I will tell you anything you wish to know."

She tore away from his grasp, standing. Her gray eyes were accusing, hurt, ripping him to shreds. "I do not think I wish to speak to you now." With the regal air of the duchess she now was, she addressed the room at large. "Thank you all for joining us this evening, but I fear the time has come for me to take my leave of you. I bid you good evening."

"Lydia," Rand and Alistair called out in unison.

"I do not wish to speak to either of you," she clipped. "I bid good evening to you all."

"Lydia, dearest daughter," the duchess attempted, trying to waylay her without success.

Lydia was too nimble, too tall, too quick. Too determined. "I must go," she said.

In a flurry of bold, red skirts, she left.

Alistair stood, not caring for appearances, not caring for anything or anyone but Lydia. "I love her, you bloody fool," he grated, glaring at Rand. "I hope you are happy." He turned to the rest, giving an exaggerated bow. "I bid you good evening."

He ran after the woman he loved. Freckles. His duchess. His wife.

Lydia.

Dear God, he hoped it would not be too little, too late.

CHAPTER 8

*L*ydia raced to her chamber, not caring that she left behind her a drawing room full of shocked family. Not caring about the stark anguish she had read on Alistair's handsome face. Each rhythmic thump of her slippers on the carpeted hall mocked her.

Lies.

The man who had proclaimed he admired her mind, who had flirted with her in the moonlight, pursued her in Oxfordshire, who had courted and wooed her with his clever kisses and his facile tongue…that man did not exist.

Lies.

A sob tore from her throat as she ran, heedless of any servant who saw the duchess crying like a little girl, hiking her evening dress about her knees to aid in her humiliated retreat. She had asked him when he announced his intentions of courting her whether or not her dowry had been behind his sudden interest. Instead of answering, he had kissed her, and she, weak, pathetic naïf that she was, had allowed herself to be distracted.

All of it, lies.

How easily she had fallen into his trap, eager for his every kiss and well-practiced seduction. But then, she would have made a ripe partridge for the plucking, considering her sparse selection of suitors and the dismal future awaiting her as a companion. And he was London's most handsome rake, with a beautiful face and the heart of a knave.

Lies.

The sorrow rose within her like a geyser, threatening to burst forth and consume her. She ran, her lungs burning, and it did not matter. He had dared to tell her he loved her. Had taken her to bed and pretended to find her attractive. His every word echoed in her mind, an endless taunt, embarrassment splitting the sorrow, smashing her heart to bits with the force of a blacksmith's heavy blow.

I am honest to a fault.

If it has never occurred to you that I like you, Freckles, precisely for who and what you are, then you are a fool.

No one else will do.

Of course, no one else would have done. Clearly, the beautiful Lady Felicity did not possess a dowry rich enough to impress him. Rage hit her next as she reached her chamber door. She had never been given to fits of temper, but one was about to claim her now. With a raw cry of outrage, she kicked her chamber door.

And regretted it instantly, for a different sort of pain than the one clenching her poor heart assaulted her, radiating up her leg. For the first time in her life, she let loose a curse.

"Bloody hell."

It felt good. It felt rebellious. It felt as if it took away the tiniest bit of the sting of realizing she had been manipulated and lied to by the man she had imagined herself in love with. She threw open the door in the ordinary fashion, limped over the threshold, and slammed it at her back. She took care to lock it and the door adjoining her chamber to the duke's. She did not require his interference whilst she packed the few possessions she desired to take with her when she left him.

Scrubbing furiously at the tears on her cheeks with the back of her hand, she paced the chamber, scouring it for dear possessions. She scooped up her books and her writing supplies first. Somewhere between her brother's shocking revelation and the moment her foot had struck the door, she'd realized that leaving Warwick was the only answer. As her husband, he could force her to remain, but since he already had obtained what he truly wanted from their union, she did not suppose he would be overly motivated to try.

The knob of her door turned. "Lydia, let me in."

She searched about for a trunk in which she could stow her personal effects. "Go away, Warwick."

He rapped on the door with enough force to rattle it. "I will not go away, damn you. Let me in so that we can discuss this."

"I have no wish to discuss anything with you, Your Grace," she gritted, gratified that she at least kept the tears from her voice. Above all, she did not wish him to know how deeply he had wounded her with his subterfuge.

"Lydia." The pounding grew louder.

She ignored it. No trunk was to be found, so she whipped back the bed coverings and robbed the sheet from her bed, laying it in the center of the floor. Never let it be said that she was not resourceful, even with a shattered heart drowning in shame.

"Lydia."

The thread inside her that had been holding her together gave way and snapped. She picked up the nearest object—a vase filled with fresh flowers, and heaved it against the door with all her might. It shattered noisily, water and glass and battered petals raining to the somewhat threadbare carpet.

Her gaze fixated on the carpet, noting it was dreadfully in need of replacement. Everything made sense now—the Spartan furnishings of the townhouse, the lack of honeymoon, the smaller-than-average number of domestics. How could she not have realized that Warwick had been pockets to let?

"Jesus, Lydia, what are you doing in there?" he demanded, sounding hoarse. Frantic.

Perhaps he was afraid she was going to ruin whatever he hadn't had to sell off prior to their wedding in order to keep his father's creditors at bay. It would serve him right if she did.

"What does it sound like, Warwick? I am breaking things." With that, she lobbed a crystal box against the door as well, wincing when it actually dented the portal. *Breaking things,* she added inwardly, *to get even with you for breaking my heart.*

"I will ask you once more to let me into this chamber so that I can explain everything to you." He gave the knob another violent turn, smacking the door with what sounded like his palm. "I have the key. Do not make me get it, I beg you."

Of course, he would have the key. She returned to the task of gathering up the things she wished to take with her. "I hope you did not send my family away, for I will be accompanying them when they leave."

How she managed to speak to him without breaking down, she did not know. Perhaps her strength was born from necessity. Perhaps from a tenacity she had not realized she possessed. Either way, she was grateful that she did not sound nearly as weak and defeated as she felt.

"Lydia." The knob twitched. "You cannot leave me, my love. Please, listen to what I have to say."

His endearment had her itching to throw something else, but despite the temptation, violence was not in her. Smashing crystal and porcelain would not fill the hollow void inside her or cure what ailed her. She felt sapped. Drained. Deflated and sad.

Most of all, brokenhearted. "I can and will, as I have no wish to hear any more of your lies."

"I never lied to you," he dared to insist.

Lydia decided she did not require another thing if it meant having to listen to any more of his nonsense. "You married me to settle your father's debts with my dowry, all while feigning an interest in me and pretending to court me. There is no other explanation for what you have done, and I will not argue a moment more. I. Am. Leaving. You." She enunciated the last with more force than necessary, gathering up the sheet and its contents and slinging it over her shoulder like a sack.

"I married you because I love you. It is true that I required a dowry, but another's dowry would have done every bit as well, Lydia." Warwick's voice sounded uncharacteristically desperate now. "I could have easily found a bride to bring me a greater fortune, but I did not want anyone else. I wanted you."

She wondered why he hadn't done as he'd threatened and retrieved the key. Either that too was a prevarication, or he hadn't the gumption to barge his way inside after what he had done.

Lydia stopped before the door, another surge of pain making tears prick her eyes. She wished its source was the foot with which she had kicked the door, but it was not. "If you loved me, you would have confided in me. And if you care for me at all in any way, you will leave now and allow me to go in peace."

The lock clicked then, and the door swung open,

revealing him. The key had been in his possession all along, then. Just another falsehood in an endless sea. His blue eyes scorched her, searing with their intensity. He stepped forward, his expression hard, lips firmed.

"You had the key," she accused, as if it mattered, this one small untruth between them. At this proximity, she could not quite stave off her reaction to him—his scent, his beauty, his body all so bitterly compelling—for as much as she knew what he could do to her, she also knew he was a heartless dissembler.

"The lock is easily picked," he countered, "and it always has been. I simply saved myself some trouble. Lydia, if you believe nothing else I say, believe this: I love you. My love for you is endless and deep as the night's sky. It is all consuming, all powerful, and nothing I ever imagined was possible before you. I believe that I loved you from the moment that I fished you from the pond, that even then, I was saving you for me, that I recognized you as my own, my other half. I love you so much that I cannot—will not—fathom my life without you in it. If you leave this night, you take my heart and everything I am with you."

His words left her mouth dry, the hands clutching the hastily gathered sheet and its contents trembling. She could not look away from his gaze, so earnest and intense. And she wanted to believe him. Her heart wanted to believe him.

But the logical portion of her mind—the part of her that believed in substance and ration and fact—refused to. She had already lost so much to him, and she needed time and distance. To be away from him, to clear her mind. "I need to go, Warwick," she forced herself to say, heart breaking all over again. "Pray do not stop me."

And then she slipped past him and down the hall, clenching her small bundle of inanimate objects to her bosom as though it could fill the gaping chasm within her.

But she knew the truth as she made her feet walk steadily away from the man she had fallen in love with. Nothing could diminish the emptiness inside her. Nor did his footsteps follow her, regardless of how much her foolish heart wished they did.

CHAPTER 9

A sennight had passed. The worst sennight of Alistair's life. He sat in Lydia's chamber, contemplating how wrong everything seemed without her, as he stared upon the gift he had commissioned.

It was a telescope, designed and crafted by William Herschel himself.

Positioned at the window she no longer stood at, in the chamber she no longer inhabited, in the home that seemed like a prison cell without her, the telescope awaited her return. Along with Alistair. A return that, given her absence of communication following her flight, seemed increasingly impossible.

The first day she was gone, he had consumed enough whisky to convince himself she would return after her temper and hurt abated. The second day, he woke on the floor of his spinning study next to an empty decanter, his head pounding, and he had realized that the whisky had made him a fool. By the third day, he'd been unable to attempt to speak with her, so he sent her a note that was returned unopened. On the fourth, fifth, and sixth days, he called upon her at Revelstoke's townhome where, on each occasion, he had been informed that his wife was not at home.

Yesterday, for the first time, Rand had appeared whilst he cooled his heels awaiting Lydia's certain rebuff. Rand had taken one look at him and whistled low.

"Christ but you look like utter shite, Warwick," his friend —perhaps former friend, given the circumstances—had observed unkindly.

"I feel like it," he had acknowledged with grim candor. "So, it is just as well that I look the part."

"I am sorry for what I said, if you must know." Rand bowed his head, studying his boots, his jaw tense. "I have been stewing ever since I found out about your debts, convinced you had made my sister the sacrificial lamb upon your altar. My baser nature got the better of me, I am afraid."

"It would not be the first time," he joked ineffectually, attempting to lighten the air. After all, he had considered Rand the brother he never had. That he had mucked up everything, alienating the two people he loved most in the world, killed him. "Will you speak with her on my behalf, Rand?"

His friend eyed him warily. "I will make no promises, but you may say your piece."

"Tell her that I love her, and that I shall wait for her, however long it takes," he said, unashamed to humble himself before Rand or anyone else. He wanted all the polite world to know that he was hopelessly in love with his duchess. But most of all, he wanted her to believe it. To believe in him again.

Rand eyed him intently, much as one might an intruder one suspected had pilfered the family silver. "You truly do love her, don't you?"

Emotion clogging his throat, Alistair simply inclined his

head. "With everything in me, and so much that it frightens me. My life without her is like a night sky stripped of its stars."

Afraid he would say more, he had gone. The ride back to his empty townhome had been silent with recrimination. Everywhere he looked, he was reminded of Lydia. Reminded she was gone, and why she had left.

Because of him.

Today marked the eighth day since he had seen or spoken, touched, or kissed his wife. The candle of his hope had begun to sputter. Unlike his father, Alistair was not—nor had he ever been—a denizen of the green baize. He did not game, did not gamble, could not abide chance. But he knew enough of it to understand that fortune was no longer on his side.

Sitting here, mooning over her, wishing she were here, would not make it so. The room still smelled of her, by God. Violets, those graceful, delicate spring beauties. Fitting she chose them as her scent, for like violets, Lydia was strong enough to withstand a harsh environment, to bloom with beauty despite all opposition.

His mind traveled back to the night she had gathered up a sheet like a peasant woman and stolen out of their home with her family. She had left him with nary a backward glance, head held high, all the way to the carriage. And he had been left alone, helpless, impotent with both rage and guilt. As much as he wanted to smash his fist into Rand's nose, he also wanted to blacken his own eye for causing Lydia the hurt he had seen in her face before she left him.

He wished he had taken her in his arms, kissed her sense-less, refused to let her leave. Now that she had, it seemed he would never get her back unless he forced the matter. But he had caused her enough pain already, more than he would have ever wished, and so he would not bring her back to his side against her will.

She would have to come to him herself. Because she wanted to. Because, like him, she could not bear to spend another day without being in his arms and in his bed. Because she loved him. And all that, he thought with a bitter chuckle, seemed about as likely as a star falling into his lap.

"Alistair."

His entire body went rigid at that voice, so mellifluous and beloved. The voice he had longed to hear and had imagined he heard in the midst of the night when he woke frustrated and alone.

Lydia's.

He shot off the bed, turning to find her standing just within the threshold of the chamber, resplendent in a purple evening gown. Silk violets were tucked into her hair. She was so lovely he lost the ability to speak for a full minute. All he could do was stare at her, inhale the sight of her as if she were air, necessary and delicious, filling his lungs. Giving him life. And she was. She did, simply by *being*. She was that bloody essential to him.

Why was she here? Hope fluttered within him, but he forced it down lest he become bitterly disappointed. He swallowed. "Lydia."

Her brother had been right. Alistair looked awful. Dark circles marred the tender flesh beneath his blue eyes. He had not shaved since she had seen him last, and a dark beard cloaked his firm, wide jaw, hiding the precious expanse of skin where she knew by heart his dimples would appear if he smiled genuinely enough. Though it had only been a week since she had fled to mend her wounded heart, his already lean frame seemed a bit sparer. He wore no cravat, coat, or waistcoat, and gone was the polished Corinthian she had come to expect.

The version of Warwick before her seemed wilder. He took two steps toward her before stopping, seeming to collect his thoughts. She knew she ought to say something—anything—but she had not quite prepared for the sensations that buffeted her upon seeing him again.

"Alistair," she returned, equally wary as she watched him.

His buff breeches made it impossible not to notice his long legs, those muscled thighs. He was so tall, so strong. She longed to bury her face in his throat, kiss the masculine protrusion of his Adam's apple, to make her way across his jaw, press her mouth to each one of his dimples. But she fell into his eyes, for they were burning and bright and greedy as they fixated upon her, and gleaming with love.

He hesitated, and ran his fingers through his hair in an uncharacteristic gesture, betraying his nervousness. "Have you come home?"

Home.

No word had ever sounded more right coming from him save *love*, and she felt it land directly in her heart like a seed that would plant itself, grow, and blossom into something a thousand times its size. She took a step toward him. "I heard you yesterday when you spoke with Rand."

He quirked a brow, still studying her as though to commit each facet of her to memory in case she disappeared. "Why did you not agree to see me, then?"

Another step brought her closer to him. "I was afraid that if I did, I would weaken in my resolve to keep you at bay."

"Yet, you stand before me, unless I am dreaming, and if

so, I have no wish to wake." He flashed her a beautiful, tentative smile.

One more step. She could smell him now, that decadent scent that was uniquely his, and she yearned to throw herself into his arms, press her nose to his chest, and inhale. "I needed to know, Alistair, for certain, that you wanted me. That you loved me."

"It is my greatest regret that I ever gave you cause to doubt it," he said, standing still, allowing her to come to him as she wished. "Why are you here, Lydia?"

"You said your life without me is like a night sky stripped of all its stars." She reached him at last, in the center of her chamber, stopped, and tipped her head back to look upon his beloved countenance. "And that is precisely how I feel about you, my love. When I left, I was not thinking clearly. I was hurt and angry. I thought you had lied to me, betrayed me, fooled me. At first, I was so angry that you'd kept your father's debts from me that I wanted to hurt you as you had hurt me. But as the days passed, I realized that hurting you was akin to hurting myself, for you are the other half of me. The half of me I never knew I was missing until I found it in you. I realized that if you did not truly love me, you had no more reason to maintain the pretense after we wed and you had my dowry in your possession. When you came to see me, and I overheard your words, and Rand told me how pale and drawn you were, I knew for certain that I had made a grave mistake."

He stiffened, his jaw going rigid. "A mistake?"

"Yes." She framed his handsome face in her hands, allowing all the love she felt for him to show in her touch, her gaze. "I should have listened to you, given you the chance to explain yourself. I should not have run from you, and I am sorry that I did. All I can promise is that for the rest of our lives, I will only ever run toward you."

His arms went around her, clasping her to him, dragging her against his chest as though he could tuck her entire being into his heart and keep her there. "And I promise to catch you, my darling duchess, just as long as you promise to do the same for me."

She rolled to her tiptoes and pressed a lingering kiss to his mouth. "Always, Alistair. Can you forgive me for leaving?"

"As long as you can forgive me for not telling you the truth of my father's debts sooner." He kissed the tip of her nose. "I would have told you from the start, but I was afraid you would think it the only reason I courted you, when the truth was that I loved you and could not bear the thought of you being any man's wife but mine."

"I understand," she murmured, for she did. Distance and time away from him had proven only one thing to her: theirs was a love that could withstand any trial, and she could not remain apart from him for one moment more. "I love you."

His mouth crushed hers in a kiss that claimed. It was hungry, plundering, and she opened to his assault, tasting him, running her tongue against his. He kissed her as if he had not kissed her in a hundred years, and she reveled in his passion and fire, clutching his broad shoulders, wishing she could stay forever in his arms.

When he broke away at last, they both breathed heavily. "Lydia," he murmured. "I love you so much. Please do not ever leave me again."

She smiled. "Never. I promise."

"Hell, I almost forgot." He spun her about so that she faced the far window and the unmistakable object standing before it. "This is your wedding gift, my love."

Awe coursed through her as she walked toward it, taking in its beauty. "A telescope," she said in wonder, trailing her fingers lovingly over its brass and wood. "You got me a telescope."

He nodded, grinning so that his dimples appeared, even beneath the layer of his beard. "Designed by Herschel."

"Oh, Alistair." She threw herself into him, looping her wrists around his neck and rising on tiptoes once more to rain kisses all over his lips, cheeks, jaw, chin. Herschel was a well-known astronomer, and his telescopes were much sought-after. Alistair must have put a great deal of thought into this gift, and he would have had to have commissioned it long ago, perhaps even before their betrothal. "This must have been very dear. You should not have gone to such an expense on my account."

"For you, I would do anything," he said with a reverence that humbled her.

"I love you," she whispered into his mouth as he bent and scooped her into his arms. "I fell in love with you a long time ago, but you stole my heart all over again one Christmas in Oxfordshire."

They kissed frantically while he stalked across the chamber, their mouths only parting when he laid her gently upon the bed.

He joined her there, his large body burning into hers as he kissed her lips, her cheeks, her throat, behind her ear. "My own bluestocking duchess, my love for you is as infinite as the moon and the sun and all the stars in the sky combined."

Lydia drew him to her for another melting kiss, and she knew she was precisely where she belonged, in the arms of the man who loved her exactly as she was, the man who loved her every bit as much as she loved him, her beloved duke.

THANK you for reading *Wishes in Winter*! I hope you enjoyed this Wicked Winters Series World book and that Lydia and Alistair made you smile. Don't miss the rest of The Wicked Winters series!

For more information on this and my other series, sign up for my newsletter here or follow me on Amazon or BookBub. Join my reader's group on Facebook for bonus content, early excerpts, giveaways, and more.

As always, please consider leaving an honest review of *Wishes in Winter.* Reviews are greatly appreciated!

Until next time,
Scarlett

DON'T MISS SCARLETT'S OTHER ROMANCES!

Complete Book List
HISTORICAL ROMANCE

Heart's Temptation
A Mad Passion (Book One)
Rebel Love (Book Two)
Reckless Need (Book Three)
Sweet Scandal (Book Four)
Restless Rake (Book Five)
Darling Duke (Book Six)
The Night Before Scandal (Book Seven)

Wicked Husbands
Her Errant Earl (Book One)
Her Lovestruck Lord (Book Two)
Her Reformed Rake (Book Three)
Her Deceptive Duke (Book Four)
Her Missing Marquess (Book Five)
Her Virtuous Viscount (Book Six)

League of Dukes
Nobody's Duke (Book One)
Heartless Duke (Book Two)
Dangerous Duke (Book Three)
Shameless Duke (Book Four)
Scandalous Duke (Book Five)
Fearless Duke (Book Six)

Notorious Ladies of London
Lady Ruthless (Book One)
Lady Wallflower (Book Two)
Lady Reckless (Book Three)
Lady Wicked (Book Four)
Lady Lawless (Book Five)
Lady Brazen (Book 6)

Unexpected Lords
The Detective Duke (Book One)
The Playboy Peer (Book Two)
The Millionaire Marquess (Book Three)
The Goodbye Governess (Book Four)

The Wicked Winters
Wicked in Winter (Book One)
Wedded in Winter (Book Two)
Wanton in Winter (Book Three)
Wishes in Winter (Book 3.5)
Willful in Winter (Book Four)
Wagered in Winter (Book Five)
Wild in Winter (Book Six)
Wooed in Winter (Book Seven)
Winter's Wallflower (Book Eight)
Winter's Woman (Book Nine)
Winter's Whispers (Book Ten)

Winter's Waltz (Book Eleven)
Winter's Widow (Book Twelve)
Winter's Warrior (Book Thirteen)
A Merry Wicked Winter (Book Fourteen)

The Sinful Suttons
Sutton's Spinster (Book One)
Sutton's Sins (Book Two)
Sutton's Surrender (Book Three)
Sutton's Seduction (Book Four)
Sutton's Scoundrel (Book Five)
Sutton's Scandal (Book Six)
Sutton's Secrets (Book Seven)

Rogue's Guild
Her Ruthless Duke (Book One)

Sins and Scoundrels
Duke of Depravity
Prince of Persuasion
Marquess of Mayhem
Sarah
Earl of Every Sin
Duke of Debauchery
Viscount of Villainy

The Wicked Winters Box Set Collections
Collection 1
Collection 2
Collection 3
Collection 4

Stand-alone Novella
Lord of Pirates

CONTEMPORARY ROMANCE
Love's Second Chance
Reprieve (Book One)
Perfect Persuasion (Book Two)
Win My Love (Book Three)

Coastal Heat
Loved Up (Book One)

ABOUT THE AUTHOR

USA Today and Amazon bestselling author Scarlett Scott writes steamy Victorian and Regency romance with strong, intelligent heroines and sexy alpha heroes. She lives in Pennsylvania and Maryland with her Canadian husband, adorable identical twins, and two dogs.

A self-professed literary junkie and nerd, she loves reading anything, but especially romance novels, poetry, and Middle English verse. Catch up with her on her website https://scarlettscottauthor.com. Hearing from readers never fails to make her day.

Scarlett's complete book list and information about upcoming releases can be found at https://scarlettscottauthor.com.

Connect with Scarlett! You can find her here:
   Join Scarlett Scott's reader group on Facebook for early excerpts, giveaways, and a whole lot of fun!
   Sign up for her newsletter here
   https://www.tiktok.com/@authorscarlettscott

facebook.com/AuthorScarlettScott

twitter.com/scarscoromance

instagram.com/scarlettscottauthor

bookbub.com/authors/scarlett-scott

amazon.com/Scarlett-Scott/e/B004NW8N2I

pinterest.com/scarlettscott

Printed in Great Britain
by Amazon

36729222R00057